JACOB'S ROAD

A run-in with the Retford clan brought Jacob Tyler nothing but trouble and grief. He found himself running for his life, until he turned and fought back. But then he had to run again, falsely accused of killing a deputy US marshal, and only one man could prove his innocence. It took a ride close to Hell and back to get that man . . .

Books by Richard Wyler
in the Linford Western Library:

BRIGHAM'S WAY

RICHARD WYLER

JACOB'S ROAD

Complete and Unabridged

LINFORD
Leicester

First published in Great Britain in 1976

First Linford Edition
published 2007

The moral right of the author has been asserted

British Library CIP Data

Wyler, Richard
  Jacob's Road.—Large print ed.—
  Linford western library
  1. Western stories
  2. Large type books
  I. Title
  823.9′14 [F]

ISBN 978–1–84617–816–0 790 1978

Published by
F. A. Thorpe (Publishing)
Anstey, Leicestershire

Set by Words & Graphics Ltd.
Anstey, Leicestershire
Printed and bound in Great Britain by
T. J. International Ltd., Padstow, Cornwall

This book is printed on acid-free paper

For Fred Nolan — who makes
things possible — thanks.

1

When the smoke had cleared one of them was down on the floor with two bullets in his chest. He was dead. The other one was on one knee by the bar, his hands held tight over the bloody wound in his right thigh. His thigh bone was broken, shattered by the heavy .45 calibre bullet, and he was in pain. He needed his leg seeing to, and fast, but he made no move, no sound. He stayed where he was, silent, never taking his eyes off the big man across the saloon, because he knew damn well that if he even coughed out of place he was liable to end up dead too, just like his brother Billy. This time they'd really bucked the odds, and they'd come off on the losing side. Ben Retford hated to admit it, but the stranger had taken them like a couple of greenhorns. The hell of it was, he hadn't even raised a sweat over it. Maybe that was what made it harder, the way he'd taken them. He'd even let Billy get his gun clear of the leather before he'd drawn. Billy had gone down with two slugs in him, then the stranger had turned on Ben, putting one more slug into Ben's thigh.

Ben Retford moved. He raised his head a little, let his body lean hard against the solid base of the bar. He wet his dry lips as he stared hard at the big man with the gun in his hand.

'Mister,' he said, 'what do they call you?'

The big man was silent for a moment. 'What you askin' for?'

'I've got two more brothers and a father. Us Retfords walk pretty tall around these parts. You can kill me, but you're a dead man. They'll get you.'

'They won't have far to look. I figure to stay over in Pueblo a spell. First off I got a meal to eat, then I aim to find me somewhere to sleep. All they got to do is ask for Jacob Tyler.'

Ben Retford realised that he was in no danger of being shot. An unarmed man would have no cause to be wary of this Jacob Tyler. He was a big man, capable of sudden violence, but he was no backshooter, no sneak-killer. He would face any challenge fair and square, giving as much as he received. He was the kind of man who scared the hell out of Ben Retford, and he knew now why he and Billy had been taken so easy.

'Anybody round this town able to doctor?' Tyler put his question to the bartender, a big Mexican with black hair and blacker eyes.

'One or two have knowledge,' the bartender said.

'Somebody better get him over to one of them before he bleeds to death all over the floor,' Jacob said, indicating Ben Retford.

There were five other men in the saloon. None of them moved. Jacob glanced around. The Retfords might have walked tall, he thought, but they didn't throw much of a shadow. He turned his gaze back on to Ben Retford.

'I walked in here myself,' Ben said to Jacob. 'I'll leave the same way.'

'Your brother figured on doing the same thing.'

Ben Retford pushed slowly to his feet. He leaned on the bar, sweat on his face. The right leg of his pants was sodden with blood.

'You've bought yourself trouble, Tyler,' he said gently.

'Mister, you pushed it. I came in here for a drink and a meal. You and the kid there figured me for an easy mark. You fancied to push me around, show me how tough the Retfords are. Trouble is, friend, I just got back from three months down in Mexico, running with a bunch so wild they'd eat you for breakfast and pick their teeth with the bones. Now I'm tired and hungry and all I want is to be left alone. You picked the wrong man, Retford, picked the wrong man on the wrong day at the wrong time. Now, I were you I'd get me over to someone who could doctor me right quick, else this saloon is going to become awful messy.'

Ben Retford turned slowly and made his way out of the saloon. He moved slowly, bent over his shattered leg, his big hands cupped around the bleeding wound as he walked. Blood streaked the sawdust spread on the plank floor, marking his passage from the saloon.

Tyler sat down after he'd righted his upturned chair. His glass of beer was still on the table and he picked it up and drank deeply.

The Mexican came from behind the bar. He took hold of Billy Retford's arms and dragged the body out of sight behind the corner of the bar and into the storeroom at the rear.

The beer glass in front of Tyler was empty when the Mexican came back. He ambled over to Jacob and sat down across from him.

'Another beer?'

'Good idea. You haven't forgot the meal have you?'

'No. May a stranger pass on a word of advice?'

Jacob smiled for a moment. 'Why not.'

'What Ben said is true. The Retfords have much power around Pueblo. They have many more cattle than all the others put together. More land. Many men and guns. Here we have no law. Only the law of the strongest. You understand?'

'I know what you mean, my friend, and I thank you for it. Only don't worry on my part. I don't aim to go looking for trouble, but if they bring it to me, I ain't running. Not until I've had that steak you keep promising me.'

The Mexican got up. He took Jacob's glass and refilled it, brought it back. He put it down, then paused, studying Jacob closely.

'You did right killing him. They are all bullies. Violent men. But they believe they are above other men. The father, Kyle Retford, was one the first Americans to settle here. He came with very little, but he took land and ran in cattle. He fought everything and everyone in his way. Always he used violence to get what he wanted. It is as much a part of him as his breathing. Even now he still uses violence to get what he wants. Nobody in Pueblo has ever tried to stop him. They dare not. His sons walk in his shadow, and his crew is the roughest in the country.'

Jacob glanced over the rim of his beer glass. 'Are you saying I should saddle up and move on?' he asked gently.

The Mexican smiled. 'Would I presume so much? You are a man who knows his own mind. And the ways of the gun are not new to you. Yet you do not seem to be a man who is careless with his life. I think you know what you are doing by staying on.'

The Mexican vanished into the kitchen behind the bar, leaving Jacob with his beer and his thoughts.

Sitting back Jacob let his weary body relax. He was tired. The ride up from Mexico had been long and tiring. He'd had his fill of being pushed around while he'd been across the border, and within two days of getting back on to American soil he'd found himself being pushed again. He hadn't asked for it, he hadn't agitated the situation, but now that it had gone beyond words he was determined not to be harried any longer. The hell with the Retfords. If they left him alone it would end there. If they didn't, then they'd get dusted some, even if they did bring him grief.

From where he was sitting Jacob had a clear view of the street. There was a thick adobe wall at his back. His rifle was propped up against his table, and his handgun, which he now reloaded, was carried on his right thigh, easily got at, even when he was seated.

He wondered for a moment just what Ben Retford was doing. It was only a fleeting thought, and he forgot it in the next moment. There were other things on his mind, things that were important to Jacob Tyler.

In his pocket was a letter, which had

chased him for months before it could be delivered. It was from his brother, Brigham, up in Colorado. And it held good news. Brig's wife Judith was expecting her first child. Jacob had smiled when he'd read the letter. It hardly seemed long since Brig had been barely old enough to ride a horse, and now there he was, the youngest of them, married, running his own spread, and almost a father. Thing was, though, that Brig had grown up fast. He had changed almost from the moment they had first ridden into the gold camp at Hope, Colorado. A lot had happened to them all. There had been trouble, a lot of trouble, but Jacob and Brig, and Seth, the third Tyler brother, had come through it, though each of them was a changed man. Brig had grown up fast, taking on a lot of responsibility, and handling it well. Seth had put on the badge, becoming Hope's first lawman, and judging by the letters Jacob had received he was making a name for himself.

And Jacob himself had saddled up and ridden out, for there was too much he wanted to see, too much he wanted to do before he settled down, if he ever did, for Jacob had the urge to keep moving. His roots never took hold, never dug themselves deep. He would stay for a while, but he was soon wanting to move on. Once things got too familiar, too routine and dull, then Jacob was liable to feel the pull of whatever lay beyond the next hill. Jacob never asked himself whether he was wasting his life, he never considered it. He liked his way of life. It suited him, and he was satisfied. He asked for nothing he couldn't pay for, worked when he needed money. His tastes were simple, and he lacked for nothing, and he knew that whenever he wanted to ride in he would be welcome at Brig's place, Seth's too. That was Jacob's way, and he was well satisfied with it.

A little later, as he sat eating his steak, he found himself being bothered by thoughts of Ben Retford and his kin.

It annoyed Jacob that he was letting himself be bothered by these thoughts. But he wasn't a stupid man, and he reasoned that if the thoughts persisted, then no matter how much he tried to tell himself he was right not to worry, there was something to think on.

Jacob finished his meal, took up his rifle and walked to the door of the saloon. He stood looking out on to the sun-bleached, dusty street. It was a street like a thousand others, in a thousand sleepy towns scattered across this wide, lonely border country. He raised his eyes, looked beyond the rooftops to the pale sky. In the far distance he could see a range of low mountains, haze-purple in the vast emptiness.

Pueblo had drawn him because it promised life and some degree of comfort after the hellhole of Revolutionary Mexico. That was all he wanted. But the feeling was growing in him that it was not to be. Jacob moved to one of the seats that stood against the wall beneath the saloon's veranda roof. He sat down, his rifle across his knees and began to roll himself a smoke. He had a wait ahead of him. After that he wasn't sure the way things might go. All he did know was that the wait would be restful and the time after would be, to say the least, interesting.

2

They came in the last hour before dark. Already long shadows lay over the hot land, black, deep shadows against the sun-bright earth.

There were ten of them. Kyle Retford was in front, a big man, heavy-boned, with powerful arms straining the sleeves of his dusty, stained shirt. He dressed like any forty-a-month-and-found cowhand. His clothing was rough, his hat sweat-frosted and old, his boots scarred and burned. An old army Colt hung at his side and a Henry rifle was in the saddle-boot. Kyle Retford was one of the old lions. A man who had never asked for anything in his lifetime and wouldn't know how to ask, even if his life depended on it. He was fifty years old, but as hard as Hell frozen over. A man only had to look at him to know that there was no use ever arguing with him, and it was plain to see that he was the kind of man used to getting his own way.

Close behind Kyle Retford rode Ben Retford. His leg was strapped up, he was in some considerable pain, but he was there because it was expected of him. Kyle would have made that ride if both his legs had been shot off and Ben knew it. If they had little else between them, there was enough loyalty among the Retfords to serve the whole Territory.

Then there was Vey Retford. He was a dangerous one. He said little, some said he thought even less, but no man would ever say it within earshot. Vey had killed men for reasons so trivial most of them couldn't even be remembered. It had often been said that he was crazy, but it had never been proved.

Will Retford was talked about as the kind of man you couldn't trust with anyone or anything. His needs were strong, always close to the surface, and no woman ever felt at ease while he was around — in the same context, men kept their hands on their wallets when they saw him coming. Will Retford liked to hurt people too. Not with guns though — his weapons were knives and his hands. He'd used both on more than one occasion.

Six of Kyle Retford's crew rode with them. They were all hard types, men who were better with guns than they were with cattle. As with all men of his kind, one of Kyle's problems was keeping the land he had taken. There was always some kind of challenge to meet. It meant running a fighting crew. And Kyle chose only the best. Years ago, when he had first started out he had drawn up the rules of the game. He didn't realise it, but his initial violence had propagated the world of violence in which he now existed, and he was only fighting against the products of his own greed and intolerance.

Kyle reined in. He hunched round and gazed at Ben. 'You managing?'

'Damn right I am,' Ben said. 'I won't give you the satisfaction of seeing me fall off this horse.'

'Whatever gave you the notion I'd want that to happen?'

'Kyle, you ain't talkin' to one of the crew now. This is me, Ben, and I know you. The great Kyle Retford. Pushing it a mite now, but still more man than all the rest of his boys put together.'

'Horseshit, boy, pure horseshit and you know it.'

Ben smiled, pleased at Kyle's reaction. He had little enough to smile about right now, and a small victory over Kyle almost made the pain worthwhile. Loyal as he was, Ben sometimes got more than a little tired of Kyle's overbearing attitude. His father had played the big man role for so long that it now influenced his every word, his every move.

Ben eyed his father now, waiting to see if Kyle took up the unspoken challenge. But Kyle had something more important on his mind, for he abruptly turned his horse about, facing the bunch of men who rode with him.

'I'll say this once. You all know I mean it when I say I'll kill any man who goes against my orders. I want this Tyler feller alive. He's going to hang, and I want him alive and able to feel that noose when it pulls tight. Let me do the talking. Just be ready to move when I say so.'

He reined about and moved out, leading his crew across the open flat that lay before the town of Pueblo.

★ ★ ★

Jacob saw them as they came across the flat. He didn't get up, or move at all. He had a clear view of them from where he sat, and they would remain in his range of vision all the way up Pueblo's main street. It was fairly cool where he sat and he had a thick wall at his back, a loaded and cocked rifle across his knees. His handgun was free in its holster.

His horse, fed and watered, was saddled and tied at the rear of the saloon, courtesy of the Mexican. Jacob had considered the way things were liable to develop, and though he didn't figure to run, it was a possibility that might present itself as the only sane way out.

Watching them ride slowly up the street Jacob let his thoughts wander. He might talk his way out of this. Then again he might not. Kyle Retford was an unknown quantity, and it was wise to treat such quantities with caution until they showed their true colours.

He didn't know what they were expecting. Confronted by a man who was obviously primed and ready for trouble might put them off-stride. Most of the so-called tough gunmen were nothing more than opportunist killers. They only made a play when everything was in their favour. Let the other men have a slight chance, maybe get the upper hand, then the gunman would ease off, biding his time, waiting until things swung his way again. Backshooting was a favourite method employed by the gunhands. Dark rooms and handy rocks provided good cover for them to shoot from. Jacob knew these facts and he used them to his advantage if a delicate-enough situation arose. He was playing a blind hand, he knew, but he had little else up his sleeve at the present.

Dust lightly misted the air as Kyle Retford's bunch drew rein. For a few short moments there was silence and an eerie stillness, broken when Kyle eased his bulk in the saddle, turning his gaze on Jacob.

'You anything to do with the Tyler's up in Colorado?'

Jacob laid a big hand on his rifle's stock. 'The same. Can't say I ever heard of you before today.'

'You'll soon hear enough to last you out.' Kyle leaned forward. 'You killed my boy, Billy. Put a slug in Ben there, maybe crippled him for life.'

'He showed sense. The other one

didn't know enough to quit.'

'Weren't no call for killin'. Sure, my boys play rough, but that ain't no call for killin'.'

'Tell you something, Retford, though you ought to know it. There's no such thing as playing where guns are concerned. Where I come from a man only takes out his gun when he means to use it. Man draws down on me he'd better be ready to take what comes. Your boys weren't ready. They figured me for somebody who'd crawl when I heard they were Retfords. Trouble is I never did worry over any man's name. It's what he's liable to do that interests me.'

Kyle Retford pushed his hat to the back of his head. 'I heard what you and your kin did up at Hope. Don't make no kind of difference to me. You come in here and gun down my boys, well, mister, there's only one way out after that. I'm going to hang you, Tyler, hang you high and let the vultures have you. What you got to say to that?'

'Sounds like a neat way of solving your problem, but it doesn't help me much, so I'll have to drop out.'

Jacob's words were delivered so calmly, so unexpectedly, that there was momentary indecision among Retford's crew. His reaction had taken them unaware. He should have been worried, if not alarmed, but here he was, talking as though he were turning down an invitation to a tea-party.

Jacob had hoped for the reaction he got, and in the few seconds he had he moved fast. He came up out of his seat easily, his rifle sliding into his hands, cocked and ready. All he needed were three steps to his right, then in through the saloon door, then through the saloon to his waiting horse and away. It sounded easy, too easy, and Jacob didn't expect to make the manoeuvre without some kind of trouble. And he was right.

He had almost reached the door when he caught a flicker of movement off to his left. Hands were reaching for ready guns, and Jacob saw danger closing in fast.

Ben Retford was one of the first to clear leather. He had his gun up and out, the hammer back, before any of the others. He fired, but his bullet was wide, for he had drawn and fired simply by reflex as Jacob had moved. His bullet dug a hole in the adobe wall inches away from Jacob, who, in turn, tilted up his rifle and returned fire. Ben Retford was knocked sideways out of his saddle by the bullet. He hit the ground hard, his yell cut off abruptly as he hit. He twisted over on to his back, his mouth moving silently, body writhing jerkily, blood spurting from the raw wound in his chest.

Jacob triggered off two more shots as he backed into the saloon. He was only sure of one hit, for his intention had been more to create confusion than to inflict more harm, but Retford's men were so close-bunched that it was near impossible to miss.

He didn't wait to see any more.

Through the door he turned and made his way across the empty saloon. The Mexican was behind the bar, a bland expression on his dark face. Jacob paused at the door that led to the rear of the building.

'A long life, my friend,' the Mexican said. 'Go with God.'

'For you the same,' Jacob answered. 'And thanks.'

'Whatever I have done — it was well worth the effort.'

Jacob went on through. The rear door was ajar and Jacob stepped outside. His horse raised its head as he approached. Jacob jammed his rifle into the saddle-boot, freed the reins and swung up into the saddle. He drew the horse's head around and gigged the animal forward.

As Jacob drew level with the end of the saloon's rear wall one of Kyle Retford's men drove his horse into sight. He had a gun in his left hand and he fired the moment he saw Jacob. The bullet caught Jacob in the left side, almost knocking him out of the saddle. Gripping with his legs Jacob steadied his mount, his right hand going for his own handgun. As he pulled it clear he saw Retford's man level his gun for another shot. Jacob dogged back his gun's hammer, swung it to bear. The Retford man fired first. His bullet burned a bloody line across Jacob's face. Jacob kicked his heels in, spurring his horse forward in a sudden lunge that put him alongside the Retford man. This time Jacob's gun spoke as he thrust the muzzle into the other man's side and tripped the trigger. Powder-smoke belched out and flame scorched the man's shirt as the heavy bullet ripped into him, through his body, emerging at the other side in a spurt of blood and lacerated flesh.

Yanking savagely on his horse's reins Jacob sent the animal into a dead run, away from town, heading for the open country towards the north. Whichever way he went there was only flat country. To the north lay hills, mountains just beyond. If he could reach them he might have a chance. He was on a good horse, a strong runner and a stayer. Jacob knew those things as pure fact. This big chestnut he was riding was a horse a man could depend on. He had pulled Jacob out of trouble more than once while they had been over the border, and Jacob had a feeling he was going to have to do it again.

He had been a damn fool to stay in Pueblo. What the hell had he been trying to prove? Jacob asked himself the question, but he couldn't answer it. All he did know was that instead of being well away from Pueblo and the Retfords, he was too close for comfort and he had the whole damn bunch on his trail, coming up close. And he knew something else too — Kyle Retford wasn't the sort to give up on a thing like this. No question about it, he was in trouble. He had to find himself a place to fight, and quick. He had a bullet in his side that was only just starting to hurt. He was bleeding too, and he needed time to tend to his wound before it put him down.

The chestnut ate up the miles gradually, but the distant hills didn't seem to get any closer to Jacob. A couple of times he glanced back over his shoulder. Retford's bunch were there, maybe a half-mile back, but they were there all the same. He had the edge on them for the moment. Could he keep it? The chestnut was a good horse but it couldn't run forever. Sooner or later it would tire and he would have to stand and fight. He knew that, accepted it, but he wanted a chance. Out here, on this flat open country he would stand little chance at all. If he could reach the protection of the hills to the north he could maybe find himself a place to fight from. The fact that he might lose out to them only crossed his mind fleetingly, then was gone. It just wasn't in Jacob to even consider defeat. It was a stubbornness that was a Tyler family trait, an inborn thing that was as much a part of them

26

as breathing and talking.

Darkness spread itself across the empty land now. Shadows grew, then merged, covering the earth. The night brought a chill to the air as the heat of the day swiftly vanished. Jacob wrestled his thick sheepskin coat free from where it was tied behind his saddle as he rode. He kept riding while he pulled it on and buttoned it against the searching cold.

The wound in his side was still hurting him. The bleeding had stopped for now, but Jacob knew it could start up again at any time. Every now and then he felt dizziness sweep over him. He didn't know just how much blood he'd lost. All he did know was that it was more than was good for him.

Time slipped by, the hours passed. The stars came out, and a pale moon silvered the land. And almost without noticing Jacob rode into the foothills of the range that promised him cover, maybe a place to hide.

Realisation came to Jacob of his

whereaboutss and he snapped out of the half-sleep he was in, knowing that he would need his wits about him if he was going to come through what lay ahead. As he guided his horse up the rising slopes his mind began to work clearly again. He needed cover. He needed time. A place where he could rest up. A good place to fight from. Maybe he was hoping for too much all at once. But each of the things he wanted fed on the others.

As he reached the higher slopes he dismounted and led his horse. The chestnut was beginning to tire a little. Jacob owed a lot to the animal and he wasn't about to abuse its faithfulness. Besides which, being on his feet kept him alert. It was too easy to relax while he was in the saddle. On the ground he had to keep moving, and it was good for him.

Close on midnight Jacob called a halt for himself. He was high up now. The rise and fall of the hills were all around him now, and he was pretty safe from any sudden attack. That much he knew, but he didn't ease his vigil a slight. Retford's bunch was still down there, and they were still coming, and he knew it.

He found a narrow stream close by and led the chestnut to drink. Jacob took his rifle and canteen and found himself a handy rock to lean against. He was able to look back down the way he had come. Somewhere in the darkness below was Kyle Retford and his crew. Jacob took a drink from his canteen, wondering what they were doing down there. He didn't wonder too long. He had things to do. He'd know about the Retfords soon enough. That was the time to start worrying about them.

Moving off again Jacob headed up the rough hill slope. Beyond where he was now were tall mountain peaks, and he knew that if he carried on in the direction he was going he would eventually reach them. Mountains would offer him better protection. A man could lose himself for a lifetime in the vastness of a mountain range. One thing was against him though. He was a stranger to this part of the country while it was possible that Retford and his crew might know these hills and mountains like they knew their own backyard. It was, Jacob realised, a notion to think on.

One way or the other, though, he was going into those mountains. The Retfords would follow him, that he also knew. Who would come out was on the other side of the coin. On that score Jacob didn't even bother to make a bet.

3

To the east the rising sun flooded the land with pale light, greying the shadows, then dispersing them completely. Faint mists clung to the sides of the high slopes where Jacob Tyler rode, and each breath left a frost in the air. He was into the mountains now, having kept on the move all night, stopping only once to tend to the bullet wound in his side. There had been little he'd been able to do. The bullet was still inside him, and Jacob knew that it should come out soon. But he couldn't worry about that now. Kyle Retford wasn't going to give him that much time.

With the coming light Jacob got his first view of Retford's bunch. They were a long way below him. Two, maybe three miles he judged. Maybe he'd been wrong, and they didn't know these mountains. Then again, perhaps they were just being careful. He'd already killed two of them. They'd all remember that before they put their hands out too far.

Jacob took a halt. He was hungry and cold and weak. From where he was he could watch the Retford bunch without being seen, for he had chosen a place where there was a stand of trees and a growth of thickets close by a high wall of rock that rose up into the clear, chill mountain air.

After seeing to his horse Jacob made a small fire and put on coffee. He had some cold meat in his pack and he wolfed this down while he waited for the coffee to boil.

He placed his rifle nearby, made sure his handgun was easily got at. When his coffee was ready he poured out a mug and stood drinking it, watching the slow progress of the eight riders far below him. They were coming, he thought, slow but very sure.

He'd been five kinds of a fool. He

knew it now, but it did nothing to ease his situation. Seth would have told him the same thing, for Seth had a calm manner that always made him think before he acted. Seth might have got himself into trouble, but he would have used his head to get himself out of further trouble. Brig, now, was more like Jacob. He had a pretty quick temper when it came to a showdown, but he was younger than Jacob, and Seth always took this into consideration over Brig's doings. His thoughts made Jacob smile. The truth was, he supposed, that he wished he had Brig and Seth with him now. Between them they made a pretty good match against any odds.

But he didn't have them with him. He had nobody. He was alone, with eight men hunting him, eight men who wouldn't stop unless they were dead or he was hanging from the nearest tree. It was a sobering thought and it snapped Jacob out of his daydreams.

He drained his coffee and turned

back to his fire for another mugful. He took one step and went to his knees as a sickening dizziness swept over him. For a while the world turned black. There was a roaring in his ears. He felt as weak as a baby. When he tried to get up he just toppled over on to his back and lay looking up through the trees to the sky beyond. He could feel himself growing cold, though there was a spreading heat on his left hand. He rolled his head and saw that his hand was almost in the small cookfire he'd made. He jerked the hand away, then made a concerted effort to stand up again. Once more he failed. Anger rose inside him at his own helplessness. He knew only that he had to get up. He had to get on to his horse and move on. Good as it was, this was no place to make a stand. He needed a better place to make his fight from.

Somehow he twisted over on to his left side and sudden pain exploded inside him. Jacob heard himself gasp — and it was the last sound he heard as the world went black on him and a silence shut out every other sound around him.

★ ★ ★

It was the odour of frying bacon that brought him fully awake. For some time he had lain in that half-world of semi-wakefulness that comes after long, deep sleep and he had wondered where he was.

He was in bed, that much he knew. He was warm and his wound didn't hurt any longer. There was a faint ache, but no more pain. He felt as if he had slept for some long hours. When he opened his eyes he saw that the room he was in was lit by a lamp and that there were dark shadows in the corners of the ceiling, and from that he judged that it was night. But which night? The night of the day he had collapsed on? Or was it the next day? Or the next? Jacob quit figuring after a minute. His questions could easily be answered when the time came.

It was plain that wherever he was it was somewhere away from the Retford bunch. If he'd been in their hands he wouldn't be receiving this kind of treatment. Oh, they'd keep him alive so they could hang him, but his surroundings wouldn't be of this kind. So who was he indebted to?

Jacob lay for a while, just savouring the smell of the bacon. He was still weak. He could tell that without moving. But he was hungry, and that bacon was doing him no good while he lay where he was.

He sat up slowly, easing himself gently from his prone position. He'd realised that his side was bandaged and he didn't want to make any move that might start his wound bleeding again.

Upright he was able to take notice of his surroundings. He was in a small, one-room cabin, with a blazing log-fire throwing heat out from the stone fireplace. There was furniture, hand-made, but well-finished. The cabin floor was wood, and Jacob saw that someone had taken great care to shape and notch each plank so that the floor was level and smooth. It was, he saw, the same with the rest of the cabin. It had been built with care and pride. There were even glass panes in the two windows. That was something not very often seen in remote places. This place had been built to last, by someone who wanted a place he could call his own.

Jacob was fully absorbed by his surroundings. So much so that he didn't see the figure move out of the shadows in the cabin's far corner. Only when the lamplight caught the figure did he notice. He turned his head, and for a moment he was unsure of what he saw, then he was certain.

A girl in a simple blue dress. She was not of more than average height, not more than twenty-three years old. After that, though, the obvious stopped, for she was, to Jacob's eyes, the most beautiful girl he'd ever seen. Her hair was long and jet-black. So black it seemed impossible, and it shone with a softness that seemed unreal. She had big, bright eyes, brown and deep that told of laughter and lightness. Her skin was smooth and gently touched by the sun. Her mouth was a soft and gentle curve. When she saw he was awake she moved towards him. Jacob could see she was slim, but with a woman's fullness to her body the way the dress fit across her breasts and the curve of her hips.

She came to the side of the bed and smiled at him. She said, 'How are you feeling now, Mr Tyler?'

'Rested some and mean hungry,' he said, then added, 'How long I been here?'

'This is your second night,' she told him. 'But don't fret none. Kyle Retford won't find you here.'

'You seen a vision that give you all this information about me?'

'No. You were pretty feverish when I got you back here. While I took that bullet out of your side you did a lot of talking. There was a lot I didn't get, but I put enough together to know what happened to you. An envelope in your shirt pocket told me your name.'

Jacob smiled. 'There you have the better of me.'

'I'm Nancy Boland,' she said.

'Nancy Boland, I am in your debt.'

'You were in trouble. You needed help.' She paused. 'I'd have done the same for anyone, though more so for someone having trouble with the Retfords.'

The tone of her voice surprised Jacob. There was a hardness to it that didn't go with her quick smile, or the soft brown eyes.

'You had dealing with them?' he asked.

'More than enough. When Ma died I was sixteen. Pa and me came to this country from Texas. We took us a little land near Pueblo, set up a cattle outfit. Not much, but Pa just wanted a chance to make a go of it. We had a few head of cattle and a small cabin. Pa hired a couple of hands. Pa's father even settled down to help us. He was a tough old man was Grandpa. Been in the border country for a long time. We thought we were all right, coming along pretty good the first couple of years. Pa made some money, built up the herd, hired more men. Then the Retfords decided we were getting too big. They started hitting us. Just little things at first, then worse. Our hands were beaten up, cattle shot, waterholes poisoned. Pa tried talking to Kyle Retford. It was no use. He tried to avoid trouble, though. Never fought back, just carried on. It went on like this for two years until the Retfords saw we weren't to be scared off. So they just up and burned us out. One day they rode in and burned the place to the ground. They shot two of our hands. Killed them in cold blood. They shot Grandpa too. Put a bullet in his leg that left him with a limp.

'They gave us our horses and told us to ride out. There was nothing else we could do. Me and Pa and Grandpa, we came here. This cabin was a place Grandpa had used on and off for years. If you don't know where it is you could never find it. We just sort of settled in and stayed. Once Grandpa was better we figured we might as well stay. There's plenty of game around, good water. Three days down the other side of the mountains there's a small town. We did fur-trapping and the like.'

Jacob watched her for a moment, seeing the frown on her face as she relived dark moments of her young life.

'But it don't end like that?' he asked gently.

Nancy shook her head. 'No. It was Pa. He began to brood. He got awful bitter over what the Retfords done to us. He took to drinking. Result of it was he started going off on his own for days at a time. He'd come back in a terrible state. Dirty, unshaven. He changed. It was horrible to see. Grandpa found out what he was doing. Pa was rustling Retford cattle, or shooting them. He even winged a couple of Retford's men.

No matter how much Grandpa or me talked to him he just wouldn't give up. It was a private war he had going. Just for revenge, nothing else, and it killed him in the end. One winter he went out and they were waiting for him. Pa had to run, but the Retfords chased him. They followed him up into the mountains. Pa must have realised he was leading them back to Grandpa and me so he took off across the mountain. The weather was bad, very cold. He lost his horse, tried to go on foot, but he just couldn't go anywhere. Grandpa found him three days later. Pa had just gone to sleep and froze to death.'

'He sounded like a good man.'

'He was. The kindest, nicest man a girl could have for a father. Until the Retfords killed all the kindness inside him.'

'So you're here with just your Grandpa?'

'I was until Grandpa died three months back. I guess he was just old. He took ill and died, all in one week. I buried him near the cabin, next to Pa.'

'And you're here all alone?' Jacob sat up straight. 'Nobody around for miles?'

'I manage, Mr. Tyler,' she said, her head coming up, those brown eyes flashing hotly at him, the mouth held in a firm line. 'I manage pretty good.'

'Now ease off there, missy, I wasn't about to say you didn't. All I was going to say was, how long did you expect to stay up here by yourself? Not for good, I hope. Why the country is full of good, honest men who'd be proud to make a wife out of a girl like you.'

'I don't intend to spend the rest of my life here, Mr. Tyler. I do hope to marry some day.' She paused, her voice faltering for a second. 'I just needed a little time on my own. I wanted to think things out before I left.'

Jacob reached out a big hand and touched her hand where it rested on the bedcovers. 'I talk too much, and think too little.'

She smiled again and the brown eyes sparkled. 'May I call you Jacob? And you call me Nancy. Please.'

'Nancy it is, and if I'm not presuming too much I think that bacon is ready for eating.'

She turned, pushing up off the bed. Jacob watched her cross over to the fire and begin to tend to the bacon.

He swung his legs slowly out of bed. He was minus boots and shirt, but he still had his pants on. He spotted his shirt then, on a chair beside the bed. It had been washed and ironed, the hole left by the bullet mended. His gunbelt was there too, and he strapped it on after he had pulled on his shirt. He located his boots beside the chair, pulled them on.

When Jacob stood up the room swayed a little. He was, he realised, still pretty weak. He was going to need time to get his strength back. If he stayed here a while he would. But just how safe was this place? Nancy's tale of how she and relatives had hidden out for a number of years in safety should have been enough to convince him.

Jacob, though, was a man who took a lot of convincing. Nancy's father had only shot Retford cattle. Jacob had shot Retfords. Two of them, and they were both dead. Kyle Retford would tear these mountains apart to find him. Jacob was certain of that. It meant that this place might yet be discovered, and if he were here, then Nancy would be in danger. Jacob would have none of that. In the short time he had known her, he had come to respect her deeply, for she was a girl of strong character, and too young and lovely to have to go through any more grief and danger. Already her young life had been shadowed by fear and uncertainty.

Jacob crossed over to the table and sat down. Nancy turned round as she heard him.

'Are you sure you should be out of bed?' she asked. She put two plates on to the table, turned back to the fire to get a steaming pot of coffee.

'I can't stay there forever,' he said. 'Nancy, I'm not too good at saying thanks, but I want you to know how grateful I am for what you've done.'

She stopped pouring coffee into china mugs. 'That sounds kind of final. Jacob, what are you trying to say?'

'I can't stay here, Nancy. Kyle Retford won't stop looking until he finds me. He could find this place, and if he does you'll be in as much trouble as I am. I won't let that chance arise. Soon as I'm sorted out I'll ride, draw them away from here. You can wait until the way is clear, then head out yourself.'

'Just like that?' Nancy banged the coffee pot down on the table. 'Do you think I don't know what I let myself in for when I brought you here? Jacob, ever since I can remember I've been fighting one thing or another. In Texas it was the Comanches and the Kiowas. Here it was the Retfords and what they did to my Pa. Everything I've had, everything I've known has slipped away from me in the end. Jacob, we've come together through circumstances that just happened but that have a common bond. I found you hurt bad and brought you here, and now you're getting better, but for two days I've sat by you and tried to help you till you were strong enough to help yourself.' Her cheeks coloured suddenly. 'I've come to know you, Jacob, without speaking a word to you, and now that you can speak I know you even more. Maybe I have no right, no right at all, but . . . I . . . I don't want you to leave me. Not ever.'

Nancy turned suddenly and rushed over to stand before the fire, her back to Jacob. From where he stood Jacob could see her slim shoulders moving gently, and he realised that she was crying. A moment later he found himself crossing over to her. He did it without conscious thought. It was the natural thing to do, he realised. He touched her shoulder and Nancy turned to face him. Tears shone on her cheeks, but she looked more beautiful to Jacob than he'd ever imagined a woman could look.

'Nancy,' he said gently, and she came into his arms, holding him to her tightly. Her lips sought his, held him, and Jacob, who had always held himself as a man who didn't need to settle down, saw the end of his drifting years. There was a feeling inside him that he had never known before, and though it was strange, Jacob realised that he would never let this girl go, come what may. They were as one now, and not even the Retfords could part them.

4

Jacob had wanted to move on the next day. Nancy, though, knew he was not yet strong enough and she had insisted on them staying at the cabin for at least two more days. Eventually Jacob had agreed, for though he wanted to get Nancy away, he knew he wasn't yet fully strong enough for hard riding.

Mid-morning of that second day the Retford bunch found the cabin. Jacob was keeping watch from one of the windows and he saw them when they rode out of the trees below the cabin. One of the riders was pointing at the cabin. A second rider got down off his horse and stood watching the cabin, and though the distance was pretty fair, well beyond rifle range, Jacob recognised the bulk of Kyle Retford.

'Nancy,' Jacob called and she came to his side. Jacob pointed out the group of horsemen. 'Go get the saddlebags,' Jacob told her. 'Don't forget your rifle.'

They had planned for this. Food and ammunition, spare clothing was at hand, ready to be placed behind the saddles of the waiting horses. All they had to do was to pick up their gear and leave the cabin by a door in the rear wall that led into a large cave that burrowed into the mountain against which the cabin was built. The cave was used as a store and stable, and from the cave a passage led out on to another flank of the mountain a mile away from where the cabin stood. It was a method that had been used often in the construction of mountain cabins, and many a man owed his life to one of those back doors.

While Nancy carried their gear through to the horses, Jacob watched the group of men below the cabin. They were still debating over some matter. Jacob didn't know what it was, but he hoped it would keep them away from the cabin for a little longer.

The extra time he'd had at the cabin had improved his condition to near normal. His side was still sore and he was still a little weak. But he knew that he'd be able to ride now, knew he'd be able to cope with almost any situation. He had to be able, this he had told himself, for now he had Nancy to think of. She was his responsibility now. Nothing must happen to her, and nothing would as long as he had a scrap of fight in him.

He heard her call from the rear of the cabin and knew she was ready to go. He turned to pick up the three canteens of water he'd filled, swung them on to his shoulder. About to go he turned for one last look through the window.

Retford's bunch was on the move. Already four of them had vanished into the brush and trees. The remaining four were coming on foot, up the rough slope towards the cabin.

Jacob hesitated. The best thing to do? He pondered. Throw a few shots at them? That would make them scatter, make them wait a while before they came on. It would give Nancy and himself a little more time.

'Jacob, what is it?' Nancy's voice came to him as she crossed the cabin.

He let her look. She watched the advancing men silently. Her face went hard for a moment, her cheeks becoming bloodless as she stared down at the distant figures.

'It wouldn't do anybody any good,' Jacob told her.

She looked at him. 'Stopping to shoot it out with them, you mean?' The hardness left her. 'I know. Just for a minute, though, it was awful tempting.'

'There'll be a time. And a place.'

Jacob turned her away from the window. The sooner they were gone from here the better. They would have a better chance out in the open. Here they were limited, and there were too many memories for Nancy. He let go of the idea of throwing down warning shots. They would have to depend on the lead they got from their head start.

Better to save the ammunition for a surer target.

Nancy led the way into the cave. On Jacob's advice she had put on a heavy riding-skirt and high boots to protect her from the rough brush they would have to ride through. A short jacket was pulled over her blouse.

Hooking the canteens over his saddlehorn Jacob made a quick check of both horses. Nancy rode a cream-coloured mare, an animal that looked like it could go some and then some more. Both horses were well rested and fidgety, ready to be on the move. Jacob helped Nancy into her saddle, handed her the rifle that had belonged to her father.

'You lead me out', he said. 'When we reach the open let me go out first. After that you ride ahead again. I'll be right behind you.'

'All right, Jacob.'

He touched her hand. 'While we ride just keep going. Only when I tell you to do something you do it. Don't ask why.

Just do it. You hear?'

'I hear,' Nancy said, and Jacob knew he would never have to tell her twice to do something.

Jacob mounted up and Nancy led them out of the cave and into the passage that would bring them out on to the opposite flank of this part of the mountain. The passage was narrow, but it was wide enough to allow a horse to pass through. Sometimes the roof was so low they had to lean forward on to the necks of the horses. There was no other sound except that of the hoofs on the hard rock floor. The light was poor and it became cold.

A good half hour passed before the light began to get stronger up ahead. A couple of times Jacob had heard faint gunshots coming from far behind them. He didn't let speculation make him force the pace any.

Nancy reined in. She moved her horse aside and Jacob saw that the passage was wider now, and a few yards ahead he could see blue sky. He rode past Nancy, keeping his rifle at the ready as his horse broke out into the open. It was very bright after the dimness of the cave. Jacob blinked his eyes as he swung down out of the saddle, and he almost missed the flash of sunlight on a moving barrel.

He did see it, though, a split second before the rifle fired. Jacob pulled to one side and the bullet clipped his shirtsleeve. He spotted the puff of smoke that followed the blast and he fired at it, levered, then fired again.

Nancy's mare came skittering out of the passage. She had her rifle out and she turned calmly and put three quick shots into the brush from where the hidden rifle had fired.

A man yelled in pain and anger. Brush crackled and popped as a heavy bulk fell foward into view. The man hit the ground in a spume of dust, rolled on to his back and lay still.

Silence came again. Jacob moved over to Nancy, helped her down. She was trembling, but she held her rifle steady.

'You think there are any more?' she asked.

Jacob shrugged. 'I don't know. But we won't stop to make a count.'

'They'll have heard those shots.'

'Yes.' Jacob indicated the man on the ground. 'You know him?'

'Name of Treat. One of Retford's gunhands.'

Jacob bent quickly over the dead man. He loosened the gunbelt and drew it off the body. He handed it to Nancy, then picked up Treat's rifle and levered out all the unused shells, putting them in one of his pockets.

'Head out, Nancy, and don't look back,' Jacob said when they had remounted, and Nancy led out, taking them into the trees that grew tall and thick on this long slope of the mountain.

They rode steadily, but not too fast, for the ground was soft underfoot. A thick carpet of leafmould silenced their passing. High above them the sunlight broke through the canopy of green in

56

dusty shafts and they rode in and out of sun and shadow, surrounded all the time by the cathedral hush of the forest.

They broke out of the trees once and found themselves riding along the edge of a great bowl. It must have been three or four miles across, maybe a half mile to its base. Steep rock sides fell away from the rimrock along which they rode and the basin was green with trees and grass and brush. Water sparkled far below. Their trail took them along the rim for a couple of miles, then veered back into the forest, easing them away from the basin.

There was a short stop just after midday. Nancy had packed cold venison and some cheese. They ate and drank cold water.

'Any sign of them?' Nancy asked.

'Not yet.'

'Maybe we'll reach Youngtown before they find us.'

Jacob recapped the canteen they'd been using. 'Don't figure on Youngtown

57

stopping them. There any kind of law there?'

'Only a part-time marshal. He's young. I don't know how good he is.'

'We may get a chance to find out,' Jacob said.

5

Youngtown nestled close to the base of heavily-wooded hills, that in turn rose into high, rugged mountains. There was good rangeland around Youngtown, and a number of ranches ran big herds on the lush grass. There were a couple of big lumber-mills just outside of town. Youngtown was a thriving place to live in. It was reasonably peaceful too, having little need for a full-time law enforcer.

Frank Cooper had been Youngtown's law for two years. The office was more or less a paper one. Cooper had little to do. He officiated at all the town's functions. He made speeches to the Ladies Temperance League. Sometimes he escorted home an over-merry drinker. When the local ranch crews came into town on Saturday nights he used to make the rounds. Above and beyond that he had little else to do. When he wasn't being marshal he was behind his workbench in the town's gunshop, which he owned.

Today, though, Frank Cooper, in his capacity as Youngtown's marshal, found himself participating in another aspect of his part-time profession. For the first time since he'd become marshal he found himself wearing a gun, and knowing a feeling that he might have to use it.

Nearly two months back he had received a letter from the office of the marshal of Hope, Colorado, giving the description of a man who was wanted in Hope for robbery with violence. The man, Noble Larch, with two others, had broken into a store in Hope. They had attacked the owner and his assistant, beating them badly. Then they had emptied the safe. Before they could get away the alarm had been raised. In the running fight that followed, Hope's marshal had shot and killed one of the robbers. One had given up. Noble Larch however had made his getaway on a stolen horse, and despite being pursued he had escaped capture. The letter gave a full description of Noble Larch and asked for any information that might lead to the capture of Larch.

The letter had been signed by Hope's marshal, Seth Tyler.

Cooper had read the letter, memorised it, and had then filed it away. But he had forgotten it, and the whole matter was brought to the fore again about a week later when three strangers rode into Youngtown. The three men hung around for a day or two. The word was that they were looking for work, and shortly after they hired on with one of the local ranches.

In the time they arrived in town and went to work, Frank Cooper realised that one of the men was Noble Larch. He was sure, for the man answered Larch's description perfectly, even down to his way of dressing, the way he wore his gun on his left hip, butt forward, very high. The identification was completed when Cooper heard the suspect speaking, for he had a pronounced stammer, and this was one of Noble Larch's known features.

Frank Cooper knew his limitations as a lawman. He had never handled a situation like this before, and he realised that it needed a man of experience. He straightaway wrote a letter to Seth Tyler, informing the marshal of Larch's presence, and asking for Tyler's help. He received a swift reply, asking him to keep Larch under observation until Tyler arrived, which would be as quickly as the marshal could settle matters in Hope.

Seth Tyler rode into Youngtown one evening some ten days later. He searched out Cooper and asked to be put in the picture.

Cooper was instantly impressed by Hope's marshal. Seth Tyler was a big man, but he carried himself quietly, speaking almost softly, though his every word was delivered with controlled force. He wore a travel-stained dark suit, a gun strapped to his right thigh, and he carried a sawn-off shotgun as casually as another man might carry a walking stick.

'You realise that Larch is liable to make a fight out of this?' Seth Tyler said.

'I've always known I might have to face this kind of situation. I won't say I'm not scared, because I am, but I won't turn my back on it.'

Seth took the mug of coffee Cooper handed him. 'Man who tells you he isn't scared is a man to leave alone.'

'How do you intend to handle it?'

'Legally I've no jurisdiction here. This is your baliwick. I've a paper that says I can escort Larch back to Hope, that's all.'

'We'll do it right,' Cooper said. 'Before we ride out in the morning I'll swear you in as my deputy. That do it?'

Seth smiled. 'Amen to the wonders of law and order.'

They ate breakfast in Youngtown's hotel and afterwards Cooper took Seth over to his shop. In his office, which served for his law work, Seth was sworn in.

The ranch on which Larch was working was about three miles out of town. Cooper spoke to the owner, who came over to Seth.

'Marshal. You want any help on this?'

'I think Mister Cooper and I can handle it. No reason to put anybody else up to be shot at. Just warn your crew to ride clear of where Larch and his partners are.'

'All right, marshal. Go careful now.'

'Larch is working over the far side of the range,' Cooper told Seth.

'All right, Frank,' Seth said. 'You ready to ride?'

Cooper nodded and they rode away from the ranch-house, turning their horses across open range. The day was clear and warm, the sky blue and cloudless. They rode steadily, not speaking much. It took them a little under two hours to reach the place where Noble Larch was working with his two partners.

The location was one of the ranch line-shacks. The three men bunked here while they did the work that had been assigned to them. The shack was built close to the creek that meandered across the range. Trees shaded the shack at the rear, and more trees lined the edge of the creek.

Drawing rein some way from the shack, Seth and Frank Cooper dismounted. They were hidden from sight by a rise in the ground, so they were able to survey the place in comparative safety.

'Three horses in the corral,' Cooper said.

'They must get their work done early, or else they're late starters,' Seth remarked.

'How do you want to do it, Seth?' Cooper asked.

'Only one way to do it. Let them know we're here. Give them a chance to walk out with their hands in the air. Those other two might not know what

Larch did. They might want to be left out.'

'And if they don't surrender?'

'Then we make them give up. They have a choice there as well. They'll be able to have it the easy way — or go the hard route.'

Cooper nodded. 'You know this kind of man?'

'Yes. I've had to handle a fair number back in Hope. They know one way of life and it's a hard and violent way. You want to handle them, then you've got to do it their way. Try any other, be a little softer, and they'll trample you down without thought.'

'I'm ready when you are,' Cooper said.

They mounted up and rode down towards the shack. They forded the creek and reined in on the far bank. It was quiet there. Smoke curled lazily up from the shack's chimney-stack. Over in the corral a horse stamped restlessly.

Seth pulled his coat back from the butt of his handgun, dogged the hammers back on his shotgun. Feeling overly self-concious Frank Cooper eased his own handgun into a more comfortable position.

'Noble Larch. I know you're in there. This is Seth Tyler. I've come to take you back to Hope. Now you know me. I play it straight. You come on out and there'll be no trouble. Cross me and I'll give you Hell. Larch, you hear me?'

There was a long silence. Then from inside the shack there was a muffled clatter. Silence again.

Seth sat motionless, waiting. Beside him Frank Cooper was wound up tight as a fiddle-string. He wondered how long the waiting would go on.

The shack door opened slowly. A man stepped out. He was tall and thin. He wore faded Levis, scuffed boots with Mexican spurs. A greasy hat was on the back of his head. He wore no shirt and the top-half of his long-johns was dirty and patched. He stepped outside and put one hand against the doorpost as if he was tired. In his free hand he held a long-barrelled .44 Colt.

'Noble don't figure to give up to you or anybody, Tyler,' he said.

'He's not doing himself any good,' Seth said.

The thin man shrugged. 'That's the way it is.'

'How do you stand in this?'

'Well now, me and Burt, we known Noble for a good long time. I guess we're with him.'

'Then you'll be treated the same,' Seth said.

'Hell, mister, that's all you say,' the thin man yelled and he put up his gun and fired at Seth.

Frank Cooper had been watching as Seth spoke to the thin man. He had wondered what was going on in the shack. When the thin man lifted his gun, Cooper was certain some kind of trap had been sprung.

Cooper was right. As the thin man opened up on Seth a rifle was poked through the shack's window and it was aimed right at Frank Cooper. Cooper reacted with a speed that surprised even himself. He grabbed for his gun, twisting himself out of the saddle in the same second. He hit the ground on his shoulder, rolled desperately while he tried to keep the rifle in sight. He never did remember aiming his gun at the window. But he did, and he fired, his bullet ripping a long slice of wood from the frame.

Seth had expected some kind of move like the one that took place. He had a feeling the thin man would make a try for him, and he was ready as a man could be. He had his shotgun on the opposite side of the horse to the thin man. Using this cover he angled the weapon in the thin man's direction and when the thin man put up his gun Seth just dropped the shotgun's barrels a fraction and tripped one trigger. As the shotgun boomed Seth felt the thin man's bullet slam into his right leg, just above the knee.

Catching the full blast of the shotgun's charge in his lower chest and stomach the thin man was kicked bodily back against the wall of the shack. He gave a terrified scream as he placed his hands over his lacerated body, as if he was trying to stop the drenching flow of blood that reddened his hands.

Frank Cooper, shoving to one knee, saw a darting figure over by the corral. The third man, he realised. Cooper turned towards the man, his gun coming up. The man saw Cooper, swung his own gun round. He never had a chance to use it. Frank Cooper fired once, then again, a third time. His first bullet took two fingers from the man's left hand. His next caught the man in the chest, turning him so that Cooper's third shot took him in the side of the head, drilling a neat entry hole, taking out the top of his skull as it exited. The man ran two or three steps before he skidded rubber-legged on to his face in the bloody dust.

Despite his bleeding leg Seth got down out of the saddle. He indicated the rear of the shack to Frank Cooper, saw the Youngtown lawman head that way, then ran for the door. Ducking low he went inside. From the gloom a rifle exploded. The bullet slammed into the doorframe. Seth hit the floor, rolled his body to one side, pushing his shotgun forward and up at the shadowy figure of Noble Larch as the man turned towards the shack's rear window.

'No way out, Larch', Seth yelled.

'The Hell, you say,' Noble Larch said.

As he faced the window he saw Frank Cooper. The lawman had his gun on Larch, but the outlaw was beyond reason. He gave an angry yell and swung his rifle round at Cooper who fired his own gun once, a split second before Seth let go with his shotgun's remaining barrel. Larch was tossed forward like a rag doll. He collided with the shack's rickety table and turned it over as he fell to the floor.

Seth pushed slowly to his feet, leaned himself against the doorframe. His leg was starting to ache. The leg of his pants was soaked with blood, but it was slow bleeding. There was no heavy, arterial bleeding, and he could stand on the leg with only a little extra pain, so there was no bone broken.

A moment later Frank Cooper came round the side of the shack. His face was pale, but he seemed all right otherwise. He'd lost his hat somewhere. There was a slight cut on his left cheek.

'You hurt bad, Seth?' he asked.

'I'll move around slow for a while, but that's about all.'

'We'd better get you back to town. There's a pretty good doctor in Youngtown.'

'I'll take you up on that,' Seth said.

Cooper fashioned a makeshift bandage for Seth's leg, then helped him on to his horse. The Youngtown lawman found his hat, retrieved his own mount and climbed into the saddle. He sat for a moment gazing at the silence of death that lay over the little shack on the banks of the peaceful creek. The place seemed just like it had when they'd ridden up such a short time ago. But there was a difference now, for three men had died in a blaze of sudden gunfire and violence.

'Won't we ever learn?' Cooper asked tiredly. 'Won't we ever learn that it's all so damn wasteful.'

'One day, maybe, Frank, but it won't happen in our time, and maybe not for a long time. Violence is part of man. It's with him when he's born. Some learn to control it. Others aren't strong enough to control it. Then there are those who trade on it to intimidate others. It exists, and while it exists it has to be fought. One way or another it has to be fought. This was the hard way, Frank. It was the only way out for Larch and those other two. Not because we wanted it, but because for them there was no other way.'

'We can call by the house on the way back. Macklin will send some of his boys out to bring the bodies to town.'

'Sounds like a good notion,' Seth said

absently. He was feeling tired, a little lightheaded. The ride from Hope had been long and hard, and now this. The prospect of a soft bed, maybe a good meal, sounded good. He hoped he could stay in the saddle long enough to reach Youngtown.

6

With the darkness came rain. At first it was only a light drizzle, but within the first hour of darkness the drizzle increased until it had become a heavy, drenching downpour.

Jacob would have kept going if he'd only had himself to consider. His thoughts now, though, centred on Nancy and what was best for her. In this darkness on this strange mountain, with the slashing downpour of icy rain, travel was a risky proposition. Jacob didn't even consider it.

He located a sheltered place in a narrow canyon. It was beneath a large overhang of rock that jutted out from the canyon wall, and it was on a slightly higher level than the trail they had been travelling.

Jacob collected wood and made a fire. He knew it was a risk, but Nancy was cold and soaked to the skin. He knew very well that the Retfords were out there somewhere. He knew it, but he was determined not to let the knowledge kill his spirit. He and Nancy were going to have to be careful, but that didn't mean they had to run and hide like animals. Jacob could sense that there would have to be a final showdown with the Retfords. When the time came he would face it. Until then, with caution at the fore, he and Nancy had to make the best of the situation.

With the fire going Jacob went out and collected more wood, making sure there was enough to see them through the night. After that he saw that the horses were fed and tethered.

Returning to the fire he saw that Nancy had put coffee on to boil. She had got out of her wet clothes as well. With a dry blanket round her she was on her knees before the fire, running a brush through her damp hair. She glanced up as he approached, smiling tiredly. Firelight shone in her eyes, turned the bare skin of her arms and shoulders to warm pinkness.

Jacob shrugged out of his coat. He took his gunbelt off and put it close by as he knelt before the fire.

'Jacob.'

He looked up. 'Yes?'

Nancy stopped brushing her hair. She made to speak then lowered her eyes for a moment. Then she got up and moved across to where Jacob knelt. Getting down beside him she took his face in her gentle hands, turning it to her. She kissed him soundly, her lips warm on his. Jacob drew her to him, feeling the soft press of her body. Imperceptibly Nancy's mood changed from clinging gentleness to demanding boldness. Jacob found himself drawn to her by his own needs, and at first he would have let himself go as far as things might have taken them. And it would have been easy. With the loosely wrapped blanket slipping to her waist, revealing her womanly fullness, Nancy seemed oblivious of her surroundings, her sparse and crude place of rest. For her there was only Jacob. The warmth of his lips on hers, the touch of his hand upon her proud breast. She held him, tightly, not wanting it to end, suddenly not caring what happened as long as she could stay with this man.

Yet it was Jacob himself who did end it, but gently, as he firmly drew her from him. Nancy gazed at him, her eyes full of questions as Jacob pulled her blanket across her firm body.

'Another time and another place,' he said, 'I'd consider myself an honoured man. Right now though, I figure I'm only too easily taking advantage of our situation, and you're too much a lady to be used that way, Nancy.'

'Place or time won't change what I feel, Jacob,' Nancy said.

'Nor me. But I reckon we both need us a breathin' space.'

She smiled, appreciating his thoughts for her, his respecting her position, and knowing that they were being wise to stop things just where they were for now.

Later, as they sat together before the fire, fed, and warmed by the flickering flames, Nancy said, 'Where do we go when we reach Youngtown?'

'Where do you want to go?'

'It doesn't matter to me as long as it's where you are.'

Jacob refilled his coffee mug. 'Up where my brother, Brigham, has his place, now that's right nice country. Plenty of good grass and water. Sort of place where a man could make himself a home. Why, that's just what Brig did. Up in those hills now, it's fine country for cattle — and people.'

'Sounds nice. So does your family. It must be nice to have family.'

He looked at her. 'Nancy, are you sure you want to get hung with me?'

'I already am,' she said, 'and there's no use you trying to talk me out of it.'

'I wouldn't think of it. All I wanted to know was if you had any doubts.'

'No, Jacob. No doubts. Not now. Not ever,' she told him, and he knew she meant it. He was glad, for it made him easier in himself, because he'd had a strange feeling over what it might have done to him if she had expressed doubts or had changed her mind.

Later still, while Nancy slept, Jacob kept watch. Somewhere out there were the Retfords. He wondered what they were doing. Had they given up for the night? Or were they still searching? It was impossible to tell and Jacob didn't dwell on it for too long. Come morning he'd have plenty of chance to see how things were.

Jacob let himself drift into a light sleep. He needed some. With daylight he would need his full wits about him. There would be no time for sleeping then. He was thankful for his ability to be able to come awake quickly at the slightest sound. As it was the night passed without incident, and with dawn greying the sky Jacob roused himself and built up the fire.

He was stiff and cold, having spent the night beside a large rock at the edge of the camp, where he had a good view of the approach to the canyon. In a while he felt better as the heat from the fire cut through the chill left by the damp night.

There was coffee on the boil and bacon crackling in the pan when he woke Nancy. Her clothes were dry now and he went to check the horses while she got dressed. By the time he returned she was kneeling before the fire forking the bacon out of the pan. She'd put some bread in with the other food and she cut off a couple of thick slices, dropping them into the pan of hot fat. While the bread fried she poured two mugs of hot coffee.

'How does it look?' she asked.

'Pretty quiet. No sign of anyone out there. I figure they did the same as us and camped when the rain came on last night.'

Nancy turned the bread over in the pan. 'How long till this rain stops?'

'Hard to say. Could keep up for a day or two. Then again it might quit in the next few minutes.'

'It'll slow us up.'

'Yes. But it will also slow up Retford and his boys. If we can keep our lead we might get out of these mountains before they do.'

Nancy put the bread on to plates, divided the bacon. They ate in silence. When they'd finished eating they had the rest of the coffee, and while Nancy got their gear tidied up and packed away Jacob put on his thick sheepskin coat, took his rifle and went off down the canyon.

At the mouth of the canyon he stopped and cast around for any sign of life. The trouble was that the rain was liable to have washed away any tracks, if any had been made. Moving out of the canyon Jacob climbed to higher ground and had a look back along the way they had come the day before. Here again there wasn't much he could see. Trees and brush lay thick all around, so he wasn't able to see far. He hunkered down and waited a while, what for he didn't quite know.

He was about ready to go back when he thought he spotted movement along the way they'd come. He watched the spot and after a minute he saw it again. Then he saw clearly as a horse and rider came into view in a clearing. Jacob recognised the man as one of Retford's gunhands.

The rider came on slowly. He didn't seem to be in any hurry. It was obvious that he was searching for tracks. Jacob watched him for over ten minutes. In all that time there was no sign of the rest of the Retford bunch. Had this man come on alone? Maybe riding through the night? Perhaps Retford had even split his men up, sending them in different directions. A lot of ifs, Jacob knew. And all of them liable to cause him trouble.

And then the rider below did the one thing Jacob had hoped he would not do. He saw the canyon, and without hesitation he turned his horse and rode over towards the canyon entrance.

Jacob thought of Nancy, and of his

own bootprints in the soft ground. The rain would not have washed them away yet. Jacob eased back into the brush and worked his way down to the low ground. He had to move fast but he had to be careful, for the approaching rider would be alert now for any sound, any movement.

The rider drew rein at the canyon mouth. He sat for a moment, casting round. When he spotted Jacob's tracks he slid his rifle free and got down off his horse.

Jacob had come down by a slightly different route, bringing him out of the brush some yards to the rear of Retford's rider. When Jacob stepped out of the brush the man was studying the line of tracks back along the canyon. Then he reached his hand out to catch up his horse's rein.

'Mister, you just stand where you are and don't move. Don't you move unless you want to die right quick,' Jacob said as he stepped out into the open behind the rider.

The man did as he was told. Jacob closed up with him, keeping his rifle levelled all the time. It had been known for a man to buck a loaded gun and to get away with it. Jacob didn't intend to give this man the chance to even think about it.

'Let go the rifle,' Jacob said, and when the man had done so, Jacob told him, 'Now take out the handgun. But do it easy, pilgrim, 'cause I'm a man who's right nervous where guns are concerned.'

The man slid his gun free, held it up and Jacob took it and tucked it away under his coat.

'All right, pilgrim, you can ease off now and turn around.'

The man was as tall as Jacob, but slimmer, with a narrow, highboned face. His eyes were small and narrow, his mouth hard, thin lipped. He returned Jacob's glance with almost a sneer. He appeared to be relaxed, as if he wasn't overly worried about his position.

'Now I'd say you were a man who was expecting his bunch to come and save his hide any minute,' Jacob said.

'I figure you'd give an arm to know just how far away they are,' the man said, and he grinned at Jacob cockily.

He was still grinning when Jacob rammed the muzzle of his rifle into his stomach. The man grunted and buckled forward and Jacob swung the muzzle again, slamming it down across the side of the man's head. The man went to his knees in the mud and stayed there for a minute, his breath coming in rasping gulps.

'Now I might not give an arm, pilgrim, but you might lose one if I don't get to know where Retford and his bunch are,' Jacob said as the man got to his feet.

There was a bruise forming on the side of his face where Jacob's rifle had caught him. The man put a hand to it and swore. He threw an angry look at Jacob. 'Mister, you can go to hell.'

This time Jacob used the butt of his

gun. It came round in a slashing arc, catching the man along his jaw, spinning him round, slamming him up against the canyon wall.

'Pilgrim, you better get the idea quick. I ain't in any mood to play games. You tell me what I need to know else I'm going to make you wish you'd never come on this mountain.'

The Retford man spat blood and a tooth. The side of his face was raw and bloody. 'Christ, mister, you like to broke my jaw. Hell, you crazy or what?'

'Crazy to stay alive is all,' Jacob said. 'Pilgrim, you know how all this came about. I don't want trouble, but Retford won't leave it lay. He made the rules, and any man on his side of the board gets in my way, then he's going to get whatever comes along.'

The man fingered his bleeding face. He looked at Jacob, and he knew by what he saw that if he wanted to walk away from this, then there was only one way to do it.

'What the hell. I don't figure it's

going to do you much good anyhow. Old Kyle, he's ready to chase you clear to Canada to get you. He's mean enough. They're about an hour behind is all.' He smiled quickly. 'Mister, you ain't got much of a chance. No sir, not much of a chance.'

'For a loser I'm not doing too bad,' Jacob said. 'Pilgrim, it's you on the wrong end of this gun, not me. Now you think on before you say any more.'

Keeping the man covered Jacob moved over to the man's horse. He released the man's saddlebags and emptied the contents on to the ground. Sorting through them Jacob took a box of ammunition, a sheathed knife and a half-bottle of whisky. Then he took the rope that was coiled up on the saddle and went over to where the rider stood watching him sullenly.

'On your face, pilgrim,' Jacob said.

The rider looked at the muddy ground at his feet and a protest rose in his throat. He never uttered it, for Jacob laid his rifle butt across his jaw again.

The rider dropped like a stone and Jacob turned him over on to his face, pulling the rider's hands behind him. Quickly Jacob roped the man's wrists together and then hauled the groggy man to the nearest tree and tied him to it securely. Before he left him Jacob emptied the cartridge loops on the man's gunbelt.

On his way back to the canyon he picked up the rider's rifle. Jacob jacked out all the shells, then smashed the rifle against a rock.

Nancy was sitting by the horses, her rifle in her hands when he got back. Jacob told her what had happened.

'Then we haven't got as big a lead as we thought we had,' she said.

'No. You ready to ride?'

Nancy nodded. They mounted up and Jacob led out along the canyon, then back on to the faint trail that led to Youngtown.

Now, Jacob knew, they had little time to linger. Retford and his bunch were close, too close. As he rode Jacob's mind worked swiftly. He wanted no more contact with Kyle Retford if he could avoid it. Contact would only mean one thing. Gunplay, more killing, and now Nancy was involved. There was only one thing for Jacob to do and that was to get her as far away as possible, and hope that Kyle would eventually tire of the chase. That was a faint hope, Jacob knew, but it was all he could do. It was all that was available to him until something better showed itself, if it ever did.

They rode as fast as they could. The rain had turned the ground to soft, clinging mud that made riding a risky proposition. The trail took them through forest and canyon, along narrow ways that clung to the sides of high mountain slopes. They crossed numerous streams and once they had to ford a fairly wide creek in full spate.

Hours slid by unnoticed. Noon came and went, the afternoon drew on, and through it all as they rode the rain fell. It maintained its steady downpour, never once slacking off, or even showing signs of slacking off.

Late afternoon found them on the lower slopes of the mountain range, riding over terrain that was more rock than anything else. Here and there the trail petered out completely, but Nancy knew the way and she took them through without hesitation.

The sky above them was dark and heavy, thick with great swollen storm-clouds, and Jacob realised that they were in for even worse weather than they already had. In a way, though, he thought, a bad storm might help them. The Retford bunch would have a hard time trailing them in a bad storm. Jacob considered, and decided that if a storm did hit, he and Nancy would try to keep going, throughout the night if need be. If they could keep their lead and reach Youngtown ahead of the Retfords they might yet keep on top of the situation.

7

The storm struck at about eight o'clock. The black night was shattered by deep-rolling thunder and sudden, vivid flashes of lightning. The skies seemed to open and a deluge of rain tumbled on to a land that was already over-watered. Streams and creeks, long since filled to their banks foamed and overflowed as more water was added to what was there.

The outset of the storm found Jacob and Nancy riding across a high meadow, with no cover closer than a mile away. Riding close to Nancy, Jacob put a hand on her arm.

'You stay close now,' he said. 'It may get a little rough. I don't want us to be separated.'

Nancy nodded, her face stark white as lightning crackled and hissed in the black sky.

'You all right?' Jacob asked.

'I will be,' she said. She leaned forward and spoke soothing words to her nervous horse.

Jacob had told her of his intention to keep going if they could, and Nancy had agreed. They might, she had said, be able to reach Youngtown by morning if they kept going.

Since leaving the canyon they had ridden without pause. Once, as they crossed a rocky ridge, Jacob had looked back and had seen the Retford bunch coming out of some trees a long way back, high above where Jacob and Nancy rode. The distance was far beyond rifle range. Jacob hadn't told Nancy. She was taking things well and he saw no reason to give her cause for worry.

As they crossed the rain-swept meadow, with the dark sky splitting with thunder and lightning, Jacob wondered where the Retfords were at that moment. He had seen no more of them, but he knew they were still following. Somewhere in those dark, cold hills they were still riding, guns ready, just waiting for the chance to have him in their sights. Jacob didn't try to fool himself. Kyle Retford wouldn't bother with a rope now. Every one of his men would be riding on the promise of a fat bonus to the man who killed Jacob Tyler. There was nothing complicated about it. He was the prey for a bunch of hunters out for blood money. And now Nancy was right in the middle of it. That more than anything made Jacob angry. They would know she was with him, but it didn't stop them. And knowing the kind of men they were, he didn't think they would stop short of killing her too if the point ever came up.

Jacob watched her as she rode just ahead of him, her back curved against the cold rain, even though she had put on the thick shortcoat from behind her saddle. She was some girl, he thought. Even now she showed no sign of giving up. And not once had he heard her pass one word of complaint. A girl like that was worth riding through hell for, and he knew that he would make the Retfords pay dearly if they caused her any harm.

From behind him came the sudden whipcrack report of a rifle, then another. Jacob reined in, jerking his horse's head round. As he turned he saw, in the lurid glare of more lightning, the strung out riders of Kyle Retford's bunch. They were still some distance away, only just within rifle-range, but they were coming on fast.

Anger jerked at Jacob's inside as he realised how close Retford's bunch was. His anger was directed at his own laxity at allowing the Retfords to get so close. He wondered how they had done it, but only briefly, for it didn't really matter now how they had done it. What mattered now was what he had to do.

Nancy had reined in at the sound of the shots, throwing a glance over her shoulder. She turned to Jacob as he drew level with her. He pulled his rifle free from its sheath, levering a shell into the chamber.

'Ride, Nancy. Just ride,' he said, 'and don't look back.'

Together they spurred their horses forward, giving the animals free rein, and both horses, sensing the urgency of the situation, took to running like they'd never known any other way of moving.

As they rode they could hear the rifles cracking behind them, but they were still beyond range. Jacob hoped they could keep their small lead. If they did they might reach the cover that lay on the far side of the meadow. There the land rose into an area of wooded hills, and it would offer ample cover, provide a place to fight from if the need arose.

Jacob let Nancy ride ahead of him, keeping his horse more or less in line behind her. He wanted to be able to cover her if any of Retford's men got close enough to do any serious shooting.

As lightning lit up the sky Jacob twisted in his saddle. The Retford bunch was still there, and closing the gap some, he saw. He considered returning fire, but dismissed the idea. He was in no position to do any accurate shooting and he had no time to set himself for steady fire.

The distance to the edge of the meadow lessened, and relief washed over Jacob as he saw the dark mass of trees and brush coming closer. Once in there he and Nancy would be able to make a stand if the need arose, or maybe even lose themselves before the Retford bunch could get to them.

And then, just as Nancy reached the first stand of trees, a single rifle shot split the night air. Nancy's horse stumbled, faltered. For a moment Jacob thought the animal would go down, but Nancy pulled hard on the reins, near-enough pulling the horse up bodily. Seconds later the horse plunged into the dark mass of brush, Jacob following close behind.

Coming out of his saddle Jacob turned and faced the oncoming riders. He let them get in close before he opened up, his riflefire raking the line of men and horses. He saw one man leave his saddle and hit the ground hard, falling in that limp way that only comes from being hard hit. He sighted again and fired, saw another man sag, then rein away, cursing loudly.

And then they were all dropping back, pulling back until they were out of range of his rifle, grouping together to add up the score before they came again.

Nancy appeared out of the shadows, her face pale, but angry.

'You hurt?' Jacob asked.

'No,' she said. 'That shot hit my horse, Jacob. Her sides all bloody and she's bleeding from the mouth.'

'You had her a long time?'

Nancy nodded, her eyes suddenly moist. 'Grandpa reared her from the day she was born. Nobody else has ever ridden her.' She rubbed her hand across her eyes. 'Look at me,' she murmured, trying to hide her upset.

'I'd feel the same way if I lost that big chestnut of mine.'

Nancy smiled briefly.

There was a confusion of noise behind them, a crashing of brush and a heavy, laboured snorting.

'Oh, Jacob.'

'I'm sorry, Nancy,' Jacob said. 'You know what to do?'

'Is there no other way for her?'

'Only the slow way, and that can take a long time and bring a lot of pain.'

Nancy turned away and vanished into the brush and Jacob watched the bunch of riders huddled beneath their slickers out on the rain-drenched meadow. They hadn't moved for some time now. He would have given a lot to have known what they were talking about.

The sound of a handgun shot told him that Nancy hadn't shirked her responsibility. Not that he had expected her to. It must have come hard to her, having to shoot the mare. It meant another link with her family gone. Maybe the last. She'd had a long run of bad luck. Jacob hoped he could help to change that run for her. When they got out of this mess, though, he told himself.

They had another problem now. Two of them and only one horse. Big as he was, Jacob's chestnut wouldn't go too far carrying double. Certainly not in this kind of terrain. Certainly not fast enough to keep ahead of the Retfords.

In the time it took to realise the situation Jacob came up with the solution. It wasn't to his liking, but that was by the way. It was the only sane way. The only common sense way to be hopeful of this turning out right for him and Nancy.

He waited for her to come back. There were tears in her eyes, but she said nothing about the incident.

'Have they moved?' she asked.

'Not yet. When they do they'll move fast and we won't have much time for talk, so listen good, because I'm only going to say this once. I'll take no arguments neither. You'll do what I say and when I say it.'

'All right, Jacob.'

'You'll find a canvas bag in my saddlebags. Put my half of the food in it and divide the ammunition up. Leave me one of the canteens and my rope. You put your saddlebags on my horse, take your rifle, and the spare canteen.' Jacob caught the gleam in her eye, saw the protest rising in her. 'Then you get on that chestnut and light out for Youngtown fast while I keep the boys out there company.'

'No, Jacob, not that.'

'No arguments we agreed. Don't make a fuss, Nancy. One horse, two people. How far would we get?'

'But we'd be together.'

'For how long? You know the Retfords. You'd just be someone else in the way. I won't take that chance. You head for Youngtown, get help. I'll keep this bunch on the run. I'll manage.

Back in Texas before the war, me and my brothers had us a cow outfit right in the middle of Comanche country and we survived that because we learned to fight the Comanche his way. The Retfords don't rate anywhere near Comanches.'

'But what if they kill you, Jacob? You're all I have left now. If I lose you, what then?' She threw her arms round him, held him close. 'I daren't lose you, Jacob, please understand. Please.'

'Then do what I say. There's no other way round this, Nancy. If there was I wouldn't hesitate to use it. This way we have a chance to come out together, and that means everything.'

She broke away from him and began to divide their supplies. when she came to the coffee she put it and the pot and mug into Jacob's bag. He'd be needing that more than she would. She also put in the whisky and the knife he'd taken from the Retford man back at the canyon. She took the bag and his canteen and his rope to where he crouched beside a tree.

'I'm ready,' she said.

Jacob put out a hand and drew her to him. He kissed her, hard, held her close for a time. He couldn't find words that might fit so he didn't speak until he let her go.

'Now you take that horse and you ride and don't you stop until you get to Youngtown. Promise me that.'

'All right, Jacob.' Nancy glanced out across the meadow to where the Retford bunch still sat waiting. 'Don't you let them get close. I want you alive, Jacob Tyler, alive and well.'

And then she turned and went into the dark-shadowed brush. Jacob heard the creak of leather and then the sound of hooves on the wet earth, and then there was nothing.

He turned his full attention to the Retford bunch. They were having a real long talk it looked like. Jacob wished they would get down to some action. At least then he would know what was what.

Casting about he surveyed the surrounding terrain. On all sides were high slopes, plentifully covered with timber. From now on he was going to be conducting a running fight. He was on foot and he would need plenty of good cover. Up in those wooded slopes he would be able to move about pretty quickly, and maybe he could keep the Retford bunch on the move too. He had to give Nancy enough time to get far away. He wanted her clear off this mountain.

Jacob slid his coiled rope up his arm to his shoulder, did the same with his canteen and the canvas bag. He filled up the magazine of his rifle, checked that his holstered handgun and the one in his belt were also fully loaded.

With these things done Jacob moved. He was as ready as he would ever be now. From here on in he was going to have to survive by keeping just that much ahead of the Retfords. He had to keep them on his trail, but not so close as to be able to touch him. One way or the other it was going to be a busy time.

With the thought on his mind Jacob stepped out of cover, showing himself to the Retfords before he turned and vanished into the trees again, with the noise of their pursuit reaching him, and the bullets from their guns searching for him out of the rainy darkness.

8

Nancy rode without pause, her only caution being a slight check on her horse's speed. She needed to make good time, but she couldn't afford to ride the big chestnut recklessly over the rough slopes that angled sharply away below her. The horse was her only chance to make Youngtown — Jacob's only chance too. If she didn't reach town and get help, then Jacob's sacrifice might cost more than either of them had anticipated. Jacob had given her a chance to get away from the Retfords, and Nancy had no intention of letting him down.

The storm continued as she rode. It showed no sign of letting up. If it did nothing else, she thought, it would at least give Jacob a fighting chance, and she knew that he would make the most of any given opportunity.

Huddled up in her thick coat, guiding the sure-footed chestnut through rain-drenched forest and across wind-swept slopes of knee-high grass Nancy lost track of the passing hours. She knew her way, so she didn't worry too much about time. But as she rode she felt weariness stealing over her. Despite her thick coat she was cold. Her face was numb from the slap of rain and the icy touch of the wind. She began to wish for warmth. A fire. Hot coffee. She thought of warm blankets, a place out of the wind and rain. She thought of these things, and then she put them from her mind. Here, now, was not the place, or time, for such thoughts. She had something to do and little time to do it in. Comfort was something that would have to take second place.

She found herself taking a narrow trail that led along the upper slope of a high bluff. The trail wound its way to the bottom of the bluff, wandering aimlessly down the crumbling face. Nancy recalled that it was a tricky ride at the best of times. Here she was going to have to tackle it in the dark, with wind and rain slapping at her all the way down.

Nancy urged the chestnut on and the animal, sensing what was wanted of it, eased its way gingerly down the wet, loose trail. Nancy, realising that the chestnut could find its way, let the animal have its head.

After some time she wondered just how far she'd come, and she glanced over her shoulder, looking back up the trail. And her breath caught in her throat, her heart pounding as she saw the dark shapes of two riders on the trail behind her. They were only just starting the descent, but they were coming her way.

For just a short moment Nancy was gripped by blind panic. She almost threw herself from the saddle, ready to run. Then she got hold of herself, forcing herself to calmness. Obviously Kyle Retford had cottoned to Jacob's plan. For a second she wondered whether they had Jacob, but she somehow knew that they wouldn't have caught him yet, if they ever would. But Kyle, being the man he was, wouldn't want a witness riding around who could tell what he'd been doing. The fact that she was a woman would mean nothing to Kyle Retford or his crew.

Nancy kept the chestnut moving. She leaned forward and took out her rifle. She levered a round into the chamber. Kicking her feet free she slid out of the saddle and led the chestnut to the side of the trail. Turning she faced the two riders, who had reined in when she had dismounted. They were still a good way off, but they were within rifle range.

Lightning suddenly hissed across the sky, lighting the black night with brilliant light. Nancy, ready, lifted her rifle. In the glare of the lightning she saw the two riders clearly, and recognised them as Retford men.

In the same moment the two riders saw Nancy, saw her ready gun, and went for their own weapons.

Nancy aimed quickly and fired. Fired again.

One of the Retford men left his saddle as his horse, burned by one of Nancy's bullets, shrilled wildly and reared in panic. The rider hit on his face, his gun going off with a crash of sound and a stab of flame. He scrambled to his feet, pawing mud from his eyes. Before he could gather his wits his horse, nervously jittering around on the narrow trail, brushed against him, spinning him over the edge of the trail. The man's yell was lost in the rushing wind as he cartwheeled out of sight, spinning helplessly down the rocky, steep slope.

Nancy had little time to feel anything over the man, for she still had the second Retford rider to contend with. He had left his saddle the moment Nancy had opened fire. He was out of her sight now, somewhere in the shadows. Nancy had no desire to get involved in a hide-and-seek gunfight with the man. She wasn't capable of it and she didn't want to waste her chances by risking a long delay.

Finding the chestnut's reins she began to ease her way down the trail, hoping that she could get plenty of distance between herself and the Retford man before he discovered what she was up to.

A curve in the trail hid her from his view and Nancy swung herself up into the saddle, urging the chestnut forward. Despite her earlier caution she now pushed the chestnut a little. Now she was beginning to feel reaction setting in. She felt more than a little scared. Her stomach churned. Her hands were trembling. She realised she had come close back there. The only thing she could do now was to keep riding. Hard and fast. Once she reached the bottom of this winding trail and got on to level ground she'd be able to force the pace up even more.

After what seemed like an eternity Nancy left the high trail behind. Before her lay a stretch of rough, undulating country, riddled with rockbeds and fields of thick, thorny brush. It was hard country, but just beyond it the land fell away in a gentle slope towards Youngtown. Nancy urged the chestnut forward, pushing the animal now, knowing that there was no time for hesitation.

Somewhere behind was the rider Kyle Retford had sent. He would still be coming, determined not to let her escape him. Nancy had stopped one of them, and she had the feeling that the remaining one would be even more determined to get her now. Let a woman get away from him and he would never be able to hold up his head in front of his friends. Nancy knew what pride could drive a man to. She knew only too well, for it had been pride that had driven her father to do what he'd done. And it had been that pride that had eventually killed him.

Later, much later, she noticed a faint greyness in the sky off to the east, and she realised that the night was nearly over. Still she drove the chestnut on, her heart going to the seemingly tireless animal as it carried her unflaggingly closer to Youngtown. Around her the day grew, throwing aside the blackness, brushing the land with grey light, then staining it watery pink. Nancy became aware of a slackening in the force of the wind. The rain began to ease off too.

Coming to the crest of a long slope she drew rein and scanned her back-trail. The Retford man was still there. She saw him riding steadily across a wide stretch of flatland far behind her, but still coming. He was, she realised, a lot closer than she had expected.

Nancy moved off again. She was so close now. She had to make it, she just had to. Taking note of her surroundings she saw that she was very close to Youngtown. Soon she would reach the trail that led directly into town. If she was right it was below her, just beyond the band of trees that grew along the base of the low hill she was on.

Relief flooded through her as she came

out of the trees and saw the trail. Nancy put the chestnut on to it and spurred him up the muddy road. Youngtown couldn't be more than a couple of miles. Once there she could seek out Frank Cooper and tell him what had happened. She knew Cooper only slightly, but she knew him as a dependable, capable young man. Youngtown's law office didn't require too much of a man, but Cooper took his job seriously and Nancy was certain that he would do all he could to help her.

A curve in the trail brought Youngtown into sight some little time later and Nancy could have cried as she saw the town's street, the buildings, showing misty grey through the fine drizzle that was all that was now left of the previous night's storm.

It was early yet and there were few people about. Lights shone from windows. Smoke curled up from chimneys. Youngtown looked sleepy and unhurried, and Nancy felt envious of all the people in the houses. For them there was warmth and comfort, the security of their own homes, the familiar duties of another day. Unexciting, sometimes dull, but still a way of life that offered more than her own did at the moment.

Frank Cooper's gunshop was some way down the street. Nancy headed towards it. First she saw his sign and the sight of it made her feel better. She drew rein and got down off the chestnut, looping her reins round the hitchrail. On an impulse Nancy took her rifle with her.

The sign on Copper's door said the shop was closed, and the door was locked. Nancy stood for a moment. She recalled that Cooper had breakfast over at the hotel each morning. Turning she stepped down on to the street and began to cross over. The hotel was on the other side.

As she walked she became aware of how tired she was. Her body felt stiff and drained. Each step was an effort, and the dragging mud on her boots didn't help any. The rifle she carried seemed to have trebled in weight.

Nancy had almost reached the far boardwalk when something made her look up, then glance back down the street she had just ridden along. Maybe it had been a faint sound, maybe a flash of colour catching the corner of her eye. She was never sure. But she did look up, and she did see, with a sudden shock, the Retford rider who had been following her. He was coming down the street, pushing his horse hard, and he had a gun in his hand.

The sound of the shot was loud in the early-morning stillness. Nancy felt the tug of the bullet as it caught the sleeve of her coat. She tried to run but her feet slid from under her and she fell into the mud. Desperately she rolled her body in towards the boardwalk, trying to make as small a target as was possible. She could see the rider getting closer, saw him adjust his aim. Nancy tried to pull her rifle to her shoulder, but her hands were wet and slippery.

Her heart was hammering, yet she felt calm, almost deliberate as she pushed to her knees and awkwardly swung her rifle up.

She suddenly knew that the man would fire first. Her one thought was for Jacob. She saw him, alone on that mountain, running from the Retfords, running but fighting, and she hoped that somehow he would get away from them.

A shot rang out, then another, two more. Nancy tensed, but there was no sudden shocking impact, no pain. She was staring at the Retford man. His gun showed no stab of flame, no wreath of powdersmoke. Like an image in a dream, moving in slow motion she saw him throw his arms wide, his body twist sideways, shuddering under the impact of heavy bullets. Blood spurted from his chest as he slid from his saddle and struck the muddy street, his limp body sliding in the soft mud.

Nancy let out her breath. She put a hand to her mouth, holding back the sobs that threatened to overcome her. She shivered with cold and with the shock that followed the release of tension.

'Nancy? Nancy, you hurt?' The voice was somehow familiar, and Nancy glanced up. Frank Cooper stood before her. He bent down to her, strong hands on her arms helping her to her feet. 'You hear me, Nancy?' he asked gently.

She nodded slowly. 'I'm alright now, Frank,' she said, trying to smile.

Cooper was saying something else but Nancy didn't hear him. She was looking beyond him, to a man standing on the boardwalk just beyond Cooper. He was a big man, tall, broad. He had a gun in his hand, smoke curling from the barrel. Nancy felt a strangeness run through her. The man looked so familiar. His build, the way he held himself. The colour of his hair. Nancy raised a hand, brushing at her eyes. Was she so tired? Was she imagining things? This man. She was so sure. But it couldn't be. Jacob was so far away.

Then the man turned his head, looked at her, and Nancy was so sure.

'Jacob?' she asked. 'Jacob, is that you?'

The man stepped down off the boardwalk. He never took his eyes off her. 'No, ma'am. Not Jacob,' he said. 'I've got a brother named Jacob. Jacob Tyler. But I'm Seth Tyler.'

9

Jacob had taken to the high places. He had gone where it would be hard for them to follow on horseback. During the night, while the storm had worn itself out, he had made his way up the dark, wet slopes, moving as fast as he could, his intention being to keep well out of their reach.

The trouble with plans, Jacob found, was that they sometimes went wrong. They didn't always turn out the way a man wanted them to.

Dawn found him well out of the reach of the Retfords, high up on a bare rock face. He was following his own way, for there were no trails up here, and by midday he found himself in a place which had only one way out, and that was the way he'd come in. That way was closed to him, because the Retfords were coming up that way.

Beyond this rim there was nothing except a sheer drop into a wide canyon, a drop of hundreds of feet. The canyon wall was as smooth as a sheet of paper. Jacob spent some time searching for a way down, but he finally realised there was no way out of this place except the way he'd come in, and that way was effectively blocked by the Retfords.

Jacob inspected his place, for he knew that like it or not, this was where he would have to make his fight from. At least there could be no attack from the rear. He couldn't get down that canyon wall — the Retfords couldn't come up it. There was little to fear from either side. He commanded the highest point where he was. The only way the Retfords could get at him was from the front, and even there he had an advantage, because they had a tricky climb up to him, most of it pretty well in the open. He would be able to shoot down on them and still keep under good cover.

That was the good part, he thought.

There was the black side to the situation. He could stand them off, probably for as long as it needed. They could sit down there and starve him out. As long as they were down there his way out was completely blocked. When they ran out of food and water they could send someone for more. He had the food he'd carried up with him and nothing more.

It could end up as a standoff, Jacob saw. With him on the rough end of the deal.

He put down his gear, took his rifle, and moved to the edge of the rim. The second he put his face into the open a rifle opened up from below. Bullets tore at the rock close by, showering him with stinging chips. Jacob drew back, getting his head down out of sight. He listened to the sound of the shots echoing into nothingness among the rock walls.

He was going to need caution to the fore. They had him pinpointed and had his range as well. Easing along the rim Jacob took off his hat and then slowly pushed himself to the edge of the rim again. He moved very slowly this time, careful not to make any sudden appearance.

Two of them were already making the climb. The way was steep and there wasn't a great deal to hold on to. While a man climbed there was little else he could do. Jacob watched them for a moment. He switched his gaze, searching out the rest of them. They were down below, all armed, all primed for action. One of them was building a fire. Jacob recognised him as the one he'd had the run in with back at the canyon.

They looked like they were all set for a long stay. A stir of anger grew in Jacob. Stay they might, but he wouldn't guarantee that stay to be a peaceful one. He eased his rifle forward, snugged it to his shoulder, aimed, and fired. His bullet took one of the climbers in the chest, knocking him back off the rockface. The man yelled once as he fell, his body bouncing off the hard rock, then he went limp as he slithered to the bottom.

As soon as he had fired Jacob switched his aim to the rest of them down below. He levered and fired as fast as he could, emptying his rifle in a blaze of fire that scattered every man in sight.

Rolling away from the edge of the rim Jacob made his way back to where he'd dropped his gear. He opened the canvas bag and helped himself to fresh loads for his rifle. If he had little else he had plenty of ammunition. They might starve him out, he thought, but they'd get themselves dusted some while they did it.

He found the bottle of whisky Nancy had put in. That would be some comfort during the night. It would get cold up here come dark.

He suddenly realised that the rain had stopped. There was little wind. He glanced up at the sky. It was clear and blue. The sun was starting to break through. It looked as though it might become warm. Jacob smiled to himself. The way things were running it was liable to get hot. Damned hot!

He reached for his canteen. He'd hardly touched it during the night and it was pretty well full. He had a quick drink, then replaced the cap. Looking round he located a niche in the rock big enough to hold the canteen. He didn't want a stray bullet punching a hole in his water supply. While the thought was in his head he put the bottle of whisky away as well.

Jacob returned to the rim again, first moving to a position even further than the one he'd used last time. He made no attempt at shooting this time. He just wanted to see what they were doing down below. The other man who had been climbing had rejoined the others down below. There were four of them round the one he'd shot. Jacob couldn't see whether he was alive or not.

Something made him pause. There were five of them down there. That was wrong. There should have been seven.

Where were the other two? Had Kyle sent them off to get more men? Or were they with the horses Kyle's bunch had had to leave some way back? Maybe they were off somewhere trying to find some route that would lead them to Jacob's position? He wondered. And then a further possibility struck him. Had Kyle Retford noticed that Jacob was on his own last night? A couple of times he had been in their sight. Had Kyle figured out Jacob's plan to get Nancy away? He might have sent a couple of his men after her. It was not hard to imagine Kyle or his men harming a woman.

Alarm roused itself in Jacob. Perhaps sending Nancy off on her own had not been such a good idea after all. If she found two of Kyle's men after her would she be able to avoid them? The chestnut was a good horse, and Nancy was a capable girl. Even so, Kyle Retford's men were hard, brutal types, professionals. A lone girl might easily be taken by them.

The more he thought about it, the more definite he became that this was what Kyle had done. Nancy might be hurt, might be running for her life right at this minute. Worse, she might be dead. The thought shocked him. It was distasteful, but it might be true. Jacob felt anger at himself for what he had done to Nancy. Because of him she might well be in bad trouble. He knew there and then that he had to find her. He had to get away from here and find her before anything happened to her. He knew that if anything did happen to her he would never be able to forgive himself.

Jacob knew what he had to do, but first he had to get away from Kyle Retford and his bunch. That was an obstacle he had to overcome. The question was how? To escape from them he would have to go back down the way he'd come. But they were waiting for him, and as long as they were there they were going to stop him if they could. Jacob saw his only chance of escape coming when it got dark. Before then he would just be inviting trouble. Come night and the dark he would still be asking for trouble, but at least he'd have a chance of dodging it. It was his only way out. All he had to do was to figure out how to effect that way.

He found a place on the rim where he could keep an eye on them without being seen. When he'd done that he set himself to thinking. It had occurred to him that what he needed was some form of distraction, something that would give them trouble long enough to allow him a chance to get down off the rim.

Above him the sun moved slowly across the sky. The air was warm, the rock on which he lay was warm. Jacob idly broke off a small edge of the crumbling, weathered rock that formed this rim he was on. Up here, exposed to the full effect of the elements the age-old rock was soft and powdery, crumbling like cheese in places. Rain and wind, ice, the searing heat of the sun, all these had combined to destroy the rock's natural strength, leaving it dead, flaking into dust.

And like one of those grains of dust, stirred by the wind, a germ of an idea formed in Jacob's mind, tossing itself back and forth for a while. He felt it might work. Then again it might not, but he had little choice. No matter how small the chance of success he had to try it. His life and Nancy's depended on it.

Jacob eased his way back along the rim to where his canvas bag lay. He opened it and tipped out the contents. Before he did anything else he reloaded his rifle and handgun and filled his belt-loops. Then he gathered up the remaining ammunition, took the knife, and began to remove the lead bullets from the brass shell cases. Each time he removed the lead from a shell he tipped the powder into his empty coffee pot. He worked slowly, but steadily, every so often moving to the edge of the rim to see what the Retfords were doing down below. They seemed to have settled down by their fire, content to leave him alone for a while. For that Jacob was grateful.

The light was starting to fade as he opened the last shell and added the powder to the pot. He saw that he had over half of the pot filled. It was better than he'd expected.

The next part was the tricky bit. Jacob took a long drink from his canteen then poured the rest of the water away. He opened the bottle of whisky and poured some into the canteen, swilled it round. Searching his pockets he found the oilskin-wrapped wooden matches he always carried with him. Jacob struck one, dropped it into the canteen. There was a faint pop as the whisky fumes ignited. Jacob lay the canteen down, letting the heat from the flames dry out the inside of the vessel. A little later, when the canteen had cooled off Jacob transferred the powder from the coffee pot into the canteen. He saved a little of the powder. Jacob packed the top of the canteen with stones, poured on a little more powder. He poked a hole in the cap before he jammed it back on.

It was getting fairly dark by the time he'd finished. Jacob sat back and picked up the bottle of whisky. He took a mouthful. It burned all the way down and for a moment Jacob wondered if it *was* whisky. The second swallow was a little better, but it was the roughest brew he'd ever tasted.

Jacob gazed at the canteen. If it did what was going to be asked of it he might get off this mountain alive — if it didn't, and went wrong, he might still get off the mountain, but not the way he wanted.

Full dark came, bringing the chill night air with it. Jacob buttoned up his coat. He slid the sheathed knife taken from the Retford man under his gunbelt. There was some dried meat in the canvas bag and he put it into one of his coat pockets.

Picking up his rifle, the canteen and

the coffee pot Jacob edged along the rim until he came to the place he'd chosen while it was still light. Here the rim rose in the form of a bald knob of crumbling stone, taller than a man and maybe fifteen feet round its shredding base. The very tip of the knob slanted out beyond the edge of the rim, hanging out into space, and it was as close as mattered to being directly over the place where the Retfords had the fire around which they were now sitting.

Jacob spent a sweaty ten minutes enlarging a narrow crevice at the base of the knob until it was large enough to take the canteen. Wedging it in tight Jacob poured some of the remaining powder into the hole he'd made in the cap of the canteen. Then he laid an ample trail of powder back along the rim a way.

Putting aside the empty coffee pot Jacob took out a match. He paused for a moment, wondering if he'd forgotten anything. He couldn't think of a thing.

He'd done all he could. All he could do now was light the match and hope that something happened.

Striking the match Jacob touched it to the powder fuse. The powder sputtered and popped, then flared into life, racing along the ground faster than Jacob had expected. He rolled behind a nearby outcropping and watched the dancing flame as it neared the place where he'd buried the canteen. Then it flared up and died. For a few long seconds there was nothing. Jacob raised his head. He wondered what had gone wrong.

The explosion was terrific. Jacob had hoped for noise, but he hadn't expected anything like the noise he got. For a moment he thought he'd loosened the entire side of the mountain. The rim beneath him shuddered and shook. The air around him was suddenly full of flying rocks. The night was illuminated by a blinding flash and was followed by the thunderous roar of the explosion. Smoke belched up in a choking cloud, dust made the air thick.

As he shoved to his feet Jacob saw that the knob of rock was gone and so was a good section of the rim. He could hear it crashing down the slope below him.

Now, he knew, was his moment. He'd have only a couple of minutes at most. Once the Retfords got themselves organised he would lose any advantage he had right at this minute.

Jacob moved to the edge of the rim, his rifle in one hand, and without hesitation he swung himself over the edge and started down the steep slope.

10

Sliding, slipping, risking broken limbs at every step, Jacob went down the steep slope in a series of bounding leaps. He hit bottom hard, going to his knees in a shower of shale and choking dust. Around him the air was heavy with dust from the explosion and the subsequent landslide of rocks, some of which were still rattling down the slope.

Jacob paused only long enough to get his bearings, then he came to his feet and moved forward. He could see little, and he had no idea where any of the Retfords were. They might all be buried beneath the rockslide for all he knew. But he had no time to find out. He would soon know if any of them were around.

He found out sooner than he had expected, for as he eased his way round a mound of shattered rock he came face to face with a big, shambling figure. The man was hatless, grey with dust. A bloody gash streaked his left cheek. For a second or two the men stared at each other. Jacob knew that at any moment the man would realise who was confronting him and he would start raising hell. That didn't have to happen Jacob realised, and as he thought about it he drove the butt of his rifle into the big man's stomach. The man grunted and buckled forward, and his face caught the full force of Jacob's rifle butt as it swung again. The big man spun away, a low moan coming from him as he went to his knees.

Jacob drew away from him, instinct guiding him back along the narrow way he'd come earlier. If he could get out of this place, out on to the open mountain slope his chances of getting away would increase some.

He suddenly found he was out of the fog of dust, with only the moonlit darkness to contend with. Jacob pushed on, seeking cover, and finding it in a stand of trees. He was able to stop for a moment, to catch his breath. Only now did he realise that the wound in his side had opened up again. He could feel blood soaking his shirt. There was nothing he could do to ease it so he left it alone.

Jacob caught movement near the place where the narrow trail led up to the place the Retfords had cornered him. He watched for a moment and was able to make out the dark shapes of moving men. They were coming, he realised. They were getting organised, following him. Jacob lifted his rifle and put a couple of shots over to where they were. He saw the shapes jerk and pull back out of sight.

Not waiting to see if they showed again Jacob turned and pushed on through the trees, coming out into the open on a flat area of grass and brush. Close by he saw the silver shine of a stream and he crossed over to it. He got down and drank deeply, rinsing the grime from his face. As he lay there he heard a faint sound off to his right. Jacob came to his feet, his rifle in his hands cocked and ready. The sound came again and Jacob moved forward, easing through thick brush. And he came face to face with the Retford horses.

He had little time to plan anything, for no sooner had he seen the five horses when he heard a shout close by, then another, and he knew that they were coming again. They had probably realised his closeness to the horses, and Jacob knew that they would be here very shortly.

He didn't hesitate, for there was no time for it. He had a short time in which to act and if he wasted it he might not get another. They could reach him by a number of ways and he couldn't be certain from which direction they might come. Jacob didn't try to figure out if he had any choice. He simply took the reins of the closest horse and swung up into the saddle, urging the animal forward into the darkness. Thick brush slashed at his legs as the horse lunged through the thicket, then he was out in the open, turning the horse towards the way that would take him to Youngtown, and Nancy.

Behind him he heard faint shouts, then the sound of shots. Jacob leaned forward over the neck of the horse, but he needn't have bothered for none of the shots came near to him.

He drove the horse on down the rugged slopes, knowing only the general direction he was headed. If the Retfords had better knowledge of this country, and he was sure they had, then they might easily get ahead of him. He could do little more than just ride, hoping to hit some regular trail before long. He was still in trouble, but at least he had a horse under him now, and that made a lot of difference.

Soon he came into heavily wooded slopes, and he was forced to slow his pace. The ground was thick with undergrowth and the tall trees cut off a lot of the moon's light, leaving him in virtual darkness. Jacob took no chances. He had a horse again and he wanted no harm to come to it.

It was well after midnight when Jacob risked a halt. He found a place where he could more-or-less hide himself and the horse, yet still keep a clear view of his surroundings. He tied the horse, took his rifle, and eased himself into a comfortable position, with his back against the thick trunk of a tree. He found the chunk of dried meat in his pocket and chewed off a corner. It was hard and tasteless, but it was better than eating grass, he thought, as he watched the horse grazing.

He planned to move on again with the first hint of light. He'd only stopped now because he felt that trying to go any farther was asking for trouble. He was in strange country, and it was too dark to go blundering around on this mountainside.

He dozed a couple of times, but he never went to sleep. The slightest sound was enough to bring him out of it, his senses alert, his gun cocked and ready. But though he heard the odd sound, reaching him out of the darkness, he heard nothing to alarm him, nothing that meant anything more than just the sounds of the creatures of the forest.

With the faintest of light filtering down through the trees Jacob was up and checking the horse over before he mounted up. He wished he had some water, for he was thirsty and he felt dirty, as if he hadn't bathed for months. He had rubbed a hand across his unshaven face, trying to remember the last shave he'd had, but he couldn't.

He mounted up and moved off through the trees. It was still chilly and he was glad of his thick coat. He rode slowly, his eyes open for any undue movement, his ears listening for any sounds that didn't fit. But there was nothing, save the subdued sound of his own passing.

Daylight was upon him when he finally rode out of the trees and found himself riding along a curving ridge above a gentle slope below which ran a faint, but clearly-defined trail.

Jacob reined in, keeping his horse well back into the shadows of a nearby high bank while he studied the trail below. To reach that trail he would have to cross a wide stretch of open ground. The Retfords could be hidden out anywhere along this ridge, or down below, in the thick brush edging the trail. Once he got out into the open they could bide their time, wait until they were ready to take him.

He sat for maybe half an hour, his eyes searching the surrounding country, and by the time he had finished, he was as sure as a man could be that there was nobody concealed, waiting for him to show. Jacob knew he could be wrong. If he was, he could only hope that he was ready for whatever might happen.

Jacob opened his coat so that he could easily reach his handgun. He kept his rifle in his right hand, his reins in his left. He couldn't do more, and knowing that he put the horse on down the slope. The day was growing brighter with every passing minute. Already the sun was warm on him. The air smelled fresh and clean. He could hear birds singing off in the trees. There was the creak of his saddle-leather, the jingle of harness. Above this there was nothing. He saw the brush moving in the gentle breeze, the grass swaying. He saw a bird dart across the sky. Apart from that he could have been the only man alive in the world.

He reached the trail and put his horse on to it, feeling relief wash over him. He kept riding, still alert, taking his horse down the trail, which wound along the side of a high bluff. It was a narrow trail, twisting its way down the bluff, and Jacob had to keep his eyes on where he was going.

It took some time to reach the bottom, and Jacob was relieved when he finally did. Ahead of him the land lay rough and rocky, the way overgrown with thick brush, the landscape given to much undulation, the earth broken up with gullys and cutbanks.

Jacob set his horse on to the trail, pushing a little now, checking his backtrail often. He saw nothing, heard nothing, and after some time he began to wonder what had happened to the Retfords. He didn't think they had given up on him. He couldn't imagine that happening, not now. The Retfords seemed to have vanished from the face of the earth, but Jacob didn't let himself be fooled by such wishful thinking. They were around somewhere. Maybe they were far ahead of him, waiting in some hidden spot. Maybe they had taken some shortcut, hoping to cut him off in some place of their own choosing. Right now he could be riding into their sights. The thought was there, but it did nothing to deter Jacob.

He was thinking of Nancy, wondering where she was. Had she been hurt? Or had she managed to reach Youngtown? Maybe right now she was doing what she could to help him, for he knew that she would do everything possible.

Of a sudden Jacob caught movement off to his left. He brought his horse round, his eyes searching, finding the source of the movement. A horse and rider. As Jacob laid his eyes on the horseman, the man fired his rifle. Jacob felt his horse shudder. It grunted and began to slow down. Jacob tried to kick his feet free, throw himself clear, but he was too slow. The horse fell, rolled, and Jacob felt its heavy weight pin his left leg as it settled. His rifle spilled from his fingers, falling out of reach. Jacob tried to free himself but he was securely pinned.

He heard a horse snort. Looking up he saw that the horseman was riding in, levering his rifle as he came. He was a big man, powerfully built. His face was badly marked with a large, bloody patch down one side, and Jacob recognised him as the one he'd hit on his way out of the confusion caused by the explosion.

145

Jacob forgot about trying to free himself. He realised that if he didn't do something very quickly it wouldn't matter whether his leg was loose or not. Pushing his hand under his coat Jacob pulled his handgun free, brought it up, dogging back the hammer.

The big man dipped the muzzle of his rifle, touched the trigger.

Numbing pain exploded in Jacob's left shoulder. He felt the slam of the heavy bullet, his body reacting to the tearing passage of the lead as it went through his shoulder and out. He felt blood dribble from the wound, soak his shirt and coat. He had no time to do anything about it, for he saw the big man jacking the rifle again, knew that he had only seconds to act. Ignoring the sickening sweat of pain that was sweeping over him Jacob swung up his handgun, using both hands to steady it. Jacob squeezed the trigger, felt the big gun slam and kick against his palm, drew back the hammer, fired again, his second bullet hitting the big man no more than a half-inch from the first.

Suddenly it became very quiet.

Jacob put a hand to his shoulder, felt the warm blood running through his fingers. He raised his eyes. The big man's horse was only yards away, standing motionless. Jacob poked his gun forward, up at the big man, and as he did the big man's rifle slid to the ground. Jacob saw the large bulk of the man, dark against the blue of the sky. The big man was looking straight at Jacob, but he looked with unseeing eyes, and as Jacob watched him, the big man slid sideways out of his saddle to the ground. The man's horse turned its head to look at its rider. It smelled blood and backed off nervously, showing white eyes and rippling its nostrils.

For a moment Jacob rested his head on his arms. His shoulder was still bleeding, badly too. He could feel it soaking its way down his back. He was starting to hurt now. The big man's bullet had made a fair-sized hole, and if he didn't do something soon he was going to be in bad trouble.

And then he heard horses approaching. Two, maybe three of them. Jacob cocked his gun, tried to place the source of the sound. He realised they were coming from his rear. Frustration ran through him, followed by anger at his own helplessness. Pinned as he was he couldn't even turn and face them. They could ride in on him and there was nothing he could do.

The horses came closer, stopped. Jacob tensed. He heard the creak of saddle-leather, then the sound of steady bootsteps. He saw a shadow fall across him. Jacob brought his gun around, tipped the barrel up, knowing that if he got the slightest chance he'd make the most of it.

And then someone said, 'Easy there, Jacob, I'm not looking for trouble,' and Jacob raised his eyes, found himself looking into the face of his brother Seth. He wondered if he was dreaming, maybe delirious, and he was certain of it when Nancy's face joined Seth's. She looked so clean and fresh and so beautiful that Jacob knew he was seeing things. He had to be. But then Nancy knelt beside him, took his face in her hands, spoke to him, and Jacob knew damn well that it was no dream. Nancy was real. So was Seth. And he was alive, maybe only just, but he was alive.

He tried to smile at Nancy, but he wasn't sure if he managed it. 'I missed you,' he told her, and he'd never spoken a truer word.

11

During the following week Nancy hardly ever left Jacob's side. He spent the first three days mostly sleeping, his body slowly regaining the strength he'd spent, and lost, while he'd engaged the Retfords. His two wounds hadn't done a thing to make his condition any better, but plenty of rest, good food, and the constant care that Nancy gave him, all helped to get him back on his feet again.

Youngtown basked beneath a cloudless sky. The season was at its hottest, and Youngtown got the full force of the sun's downpour. It became almost too hot to move around. The air stifled, and just thinking about moving seemed to make a man sweat.

Seth Tyler spent most of his time taking slow rides on the outskirts of town. He told Jacob he was exercising his leg, getting used to being in the saddle again. This was partly true. But Seth's main reason for his daily rides was something far beyond merely exercising a stiff leg. Seth was keeping his eyes open for the appearance of the Retfords. In any form, whether it was in a bunch, or just one man come to figure out the lay of the land.

What he'd learned from both Nancy and Frank Cooper was enough to let him know that the Retford bunch wouldn't give up. Not now, not ever. The age-old ritual of family vengeance, eye-for-eye, was too much a part of this country to ever be brushed aside lightly. The fact that Jacob had whittled the Retfords down to practically zero meant nothing. As long as there was one of them left it would never be over. To Seth it was a senseless code of living, but for all that, he knew the situation to be deadly in the extreme. It was clear and simple — Kyle Retford wanted Jacob dead, and he would try to achieve that end no matter what it cost.

Four days back Seth had sent off a letter to Brigham, explaining the situation, and asking Brig to send down a couple of his men. Seth and Jacob needed help, and Seth wasn't so proud that he couldn't ask for it. Just what they were going to have to face when the Retfords came, he didn't know, but whatever it was he wanted to be prepared.

Frank Cooper had taken them into his house, and he and his young wife had done everything they could to make things easy for Jacob. Cooper had made it clear that he would stand by them if trouble came, but Seth — speaking for Jacob as well — said that he had no intention of bringing trouble into Youngtown. The fight was a personal thing between the Retfords and Seth and Jacob, and there was no justification in allowing the people of Youngtown to get involved. Cooper had said no more on the matter, but Seth knew that the lawman was ready to make a stand if trouble did come. Seth began to hope that Brig acted on his letter fast, so that he could get Jacob and Nancy out of Youngtown.

By the end of the first week Jacob was able to sit up and take notice. He was still pretty weak, and Seth realised it was going to be some time before Jacob would be able to ride back to Hope. Seth kept off the subject of the Retfords, and Nancy, noticing his approach, wisely followed suit. Jacob soon realised he was being put off, however. He knew damn well that Seth had something up his sleeve, but Seth wasn't talking. Jacob let it go, for he knew that if things did start to happen Seth would let him in on things more than soon enough.

He let himself relax, enjoying the pampering Nancy afforded him, knowing that once he was back on his feet there would be little time for such luxuries. He had to admit to himself that he was still feeling under the mark. He tired easily, and he had little strength. But his appetite increased with each day that passed, and Jacob knew that to be a sign he was getting better.

The days drifted by. For the people of Youngtown life carried on its normal course. Little that was out of the ordinary took place. That was until one hazy afternoon when two men rode into town, dismounted outside the saloon and went in.

Seth was on the boardwalk outside Frank Cooper's gunshop. He was sitting on the long bench against the shop front. To any eye he looked to be asleep, just a lazy man doing some time-wasting in the hot sun. Nothing could have been further from the truth. There hadn't been a thing that had happened on the street that he hadn't seen all the while he'd been there.

He watched the two riders come in, go into the saloon. Seth got up and went into the shop.

'Frank,' he said, 'do something for me.'

Cooper glanced up from his bench.

He saw the look on Seth's face. 'I smell trouble.'

'I could be wrong,' Seth told him. 'Two men just rode in. Strangers I'd say. I read them as hired-guns. They're in the saloon. Like you to take a look. See if you know them.'

Cooper picked up his hat and went out of the shop. Through the gunshop window, Seth watched him go down the street and into the saloon.

'You think Kyle Retford sent them?'

Seth turned. Nancy was in the doorway that led into the living quarters in back of the shop. Her face reflected her concern, as if she were saying to herself, Here it is. Now it starts again.

'Hey, there, don't you stand around creasing up that pretty face like that.'

'Was I?' she asked. She came into the shop, stared through the window. 'Are you going to tell Jacob?'

'No.' Seth leaned against the wall, his eyes on the saloon down the street. 'I don't see any profit in telling him. If he knows there may be a couple of Retford's hired-guns out there he's just liable to get up and go after them in his nightshirt. And he just isn't well enough.'

'It would have been quicker to say, 'Nancy, don't tell him'.'

Seth smiled. 'I guess it would.'

They saw Frank Cooper come out of the saloon. Seth stepped outside and met him on the boardwalk. Cooper looked grimly serious as he took off his hat and ran his kerchief round the sweatband.

'You were right, Seth. I know their faces. Heard tell about them too. Yancy Corbin and Jay Sudbrac. They've got pretty grim reputations down around this part of the country. The saying is if a man can meet their price, then they'll go after anyone. And they were asking around after a man and a girl riding together, and the description fits Nancy and Jacob.'

Seth raised his eyes towards the saloon. As he did Corbin and Sudbrac walked out of the saloon. They stood on the boardwalk, shadowed by the saloon's veranda roof.

'What can we do?' Cooper asked. He stepped up beside Seth, his hand close to the gun he wore.

'Stay out of this, Frank,' Seth said, and before Cooper could say a word, Seth stepped off the boardwalk and started across the street.

Jay Sudbrac came to the edge of the saloon boardwalk and watched Seth walking across the street. He sensed something in the way the big man walked, and he drew Corbin to his side with a flick of his hand.

'You know him?' Corbin asked.

'He fits Tyler's description pretty good,' Sudbrac said.

'Maybe. But his health is too good for a shot-up man.'

'You figure he's kin?'

Corbin shrugged. 'He gets in the way it'll make the family two short.'

Sudbrac laughed menacingly.

Seth stopped about twelve feet from

the boardwalk. He put his gaze from one to the other before he spoke.

'Kyle Retford must be getting short of funds if he has to hire scum like you to do his dirty work.'

Anger coloured Yancy Corbin's unshaven face. 'Mister, I don't know who you are, but I'll be finding out when I read your tombstone.'

'Name's Seth Tyler. Brother of the man Kyle Retford's paying you to most probably backshoot. You're Corbin and Sudbrac, and I'm going to give you no time at all to go for your guns before I start shooting.'

Sudbrac threw a hasty glance at Corbin. He was confused, angry, and for the first time in his life he was unsure of himself. It was a feeling that only lasted for a few seconds, for as he looked at Yancy he saw that his partner was already going for his gun, and Sudbrac knew suddenly that Seth Tyler was not trying to bluff them. His challenge was real and final, and there was only one way out of it. Jay Sudbrac went for his gun, felt it slide free, sensed the hammer going back beneath his thumb. He arced the gun up, knowing that it would line up on Tyler, and in seconds it would all be over.

The first shot cleaved the hot air, followed by a second, then four more, all close, the separate sounds merging into one rolling crackle.

In the instant of the first shot Jay Sudbrac felt a savage blow strike his chest. Pain followed it, pain so strong it numbed him, stopping him even crying out. He felt himself pushed back by an invisible hand. He turned on his heel and thrust out his hands as he felt himself falling, but he had no control and he plunged headfirst through the saloon's painted and gilded front window.

As his bullet hit Sudbrac, Seth turned slightly, dropping into a crouch as his gun lined up on Yancy Corbin, but as he turned, his still-weak leg gave way under him and he fell sideways. As it was the fall saved him from Corbin's first shot. Seth let himself fall, then rolled, coming round on to his stomach, pushing his cocked gun forward, tilting it up. He saw Corbin, saw the gunman's moving weapon, knew it would only be a second before Corbin fired. Tripping his trigger Seth dogged back the hammer and fired again, then a third time, and on the heels of his third shot Corbin's gun discharged, the bullet ploughing into the dirt close by Seth's left hip. Then Corbin was down, his gun spilling from his fingers as he fell on to his face, sliding limply down the steps onto the dusty street.

Seth got up slowly. His leg was aching. He began to reload his gun as Frank Cooper joined him, with Nancy close behind.

'Seth, you hurt?' Cooper asked.

Seth shook his head. He put his gun away, went over to where Corbin lay and checked to see if he was still alive. But Corbin was dead, and so was Sudbrac when Seth had a look at him.

'Now you can see why I don't want

to bring Retford into Youngtown. We were lucky this time. There were only two of them. Next time it could be a dozen, maybe more. Retford is mean enough to burn this town to the ground to get what he wants.'

Seth walked back towards the gun-shop, limping slightly. Nancy followed him, looking back over her shoulder at the crowd that was gathering around the two bodies. She shivered despite the heat. Suddenly she wanted to leave Youngtown, to get away from this part of the country altogether, although she knew that doing so wouldn't solve the problem. Kyle Retford was the kind of man who had a long arm, and it would reach far.

12

Brigham Tyler rode into Youngtown two days after Seth's shoot-out with Sudbrac and Corbin. He rode in just before noon, and he was alone. Reining in before Frank Cooper's place he dismounted and was in the act of removing his saddlebags when Seth stepped out on to the boardwalk.

'Brig, you look tired,' Seth remarked.

Brigham stroked his unshaven face. 'I feel it,' he said. 'That's no Sunday-morning ride down from Hope.'

'Hot and dry,' Seth smiled.

Brigham nodded. 'And some.' He stepped up on to the boardwalk. 'How's Jacob?'

'Better. Still weak, though.'

'Your leg?'

Seth shrugged. 'Doc figures it ain't going to fall off after all,' he said.

'Looks like I'm the only one fit to be

on my feet. And I ain't feeling too spritely at the present. Hope this Retford feller holds off 'til I get some sleep.'

Seth led the way into the rear of the store, taking Brigham to Jacob's room. Jacob was sitting up in bed, Nancy sitting on a hard-backed chair beside the bed.

'Hey, Brig, how are you, boy,' Jacob grinned as Brigham came into the room.

After introductions had been made Brigham sat on the edge of Jacob's bed. He shook his head slowly at Jacob in mock reproof. 'Always did say you weren't growed enough to leave home on your own.'

'Brig, I damn well wish I hadn't.'

'Man, I reckon this Retford feller wishes the same by now. I reckon you must have just about wiped him out.'

Nancy said, 'As long as he can hire men and guns he won't ever be finished. Kyle Retford is a vengeful man. Jacob's done more to him than any man living and he'll never let it lie.'

'Jacob,' Seth said, and when his brother glanced at him, he went on, 'I had Brig contact the U.S. Marshal's Office before he came down here. Figured maybe we could use a little official help on this.'

Jacob's face hardened for a moment, and it seemed that he was about to have words with Seth. Then he visibly relaxed. A quick smile touched his face. 'One time I might have been mad at that idea. What the hell, Seth, there's been enough bloodshed over this damned affair. I don't want any more. If somebody can get Retford to see sense I'll back up any play he wants to make.'

Seth caught Brigham's eye and a look of relief passed between them. They both knew Jacob's quick temper, his opposition to outside interference in personal matters. Jacob was a loner, a man who sorted out his own problems his own way. But he wasn't a stupid man, and there comes a time when even independence has to give way to outside influence.

'I'd better get cleaned up,' Brigham said.

His words broke the silence that had descended. Seth followed Brigham out of the room, leaving Nancy alone with Jacob.

After a moment she leaned over and kissed him gently on the cheek.

'For what?' Jacob asked.

'Diplomacy,' Nancy said. 'You were boiling mad because Seth sent for the marshal, but you eased off.'

'Seth was right. This thing could go on for ever if we left it to Kyle Retford. Always was Seth who sat and figured out the sensible way to solve a problem.'

'You're a lucky man, Jacob. Must be nice to belong to a family like yours. People always there to help when you need it. No questions asked. No criticism. Just help.'

'Hey, you forgetting something?'

Nancy glanced at him. 'What?'

'You're part of that family now, and don't you ever worry about having to wait for help. You hear? Not ever.'

Nancy nodded. 'Yes, Jacob. I do hear.'

She stayed with him for a little longer, then left him so he could rest. In the kitchen she found Brigham, now washed and shaved, having a meal. Seth was there too. He brought her a mug of coffee as she sat down.

'Any idea when the marshal might arrive?' Nancy asked.

Brigham glanced up from his plate. 'He won't be coming here,' he told her. 'We arranged to meet up at Blanco Station.'

'It's a stage-stop,' Seth said, 'just below the border with Colorado. Marshal will be coming in on the stage from Amarillo. They're sending a man named Alvin LeRoy. I've heard about him. He's a good man. I figure he should be able to give us some sound help.'

'Oh, I hope so,' Nancy said. Her

voice was suddenly very small and forlorn.

Brigham reached out a hand and touched her arm. 'Easy now, Nancy, it ain't all darkness. We'll come out of this walking tall, you take my word.'

Nancy smiled. 'I ... I hear that you're waiting to become a proud father.'

Seth gave an almost apologetic cough. 'Hell, Brig, I forgot to ask. How's Judith coming along?'

Brigham grinned then, his eyes lighting up with pleasure. 'It's already over,' he said. 'We had a son a week ago. Seth, you're an uncle.'

Seth smiled. 'Well hell, Brig, you beat us all.'

When Jacob heard the news he was delighted. He didn't seem to be able to get over it. Every time he looked at Brigham he would smile gently and shake his head. The thought of being an uncle tickled him, too. It was a side to Jacob that few had ever seen before, Brigham and Seth included. Jacob was still trying to adjust to the fact that his younger brother was now a father when they all rode out of Youngtown two days later.

They headed north, taking the trail that would eventually bring them to the stage-stop at Blanco Station. Though none of them knew it there and then, it was going to be a time in their lives that none of them would ever forget.

As the Tylers rode out of Youngtown, aiming for Blanco Station, a lone rider rode away from town. He drove his horse hard and fast as he took the news to Kyle Retford that the quarry was on the move.

13

The ride was long and hard. They were passing through dry, harsh territory; the land supported little, mostly cactus and mesquite. On the higher ground there was palo verde and catclaw. Sometimes the dusty soil gave way to stretches of barren lavabeds, tortured layers of once molten rock turned black and brittle. Here there was little; clumps of cholla grass and bisnaga, little else. They would ride over these islands of rock until they were able to get back on to the comparative softness of the near desertland that stretched endlessly around them. Above them by day the sun bore down without let up, and at night they sat around their fire, staving out the chill with hot coffee.

Through the first few days they talked and laughed against the oppressive silence of the vast land. But the talk and the laughter faded, and they found that it was easier to just concentrate on the job in hand. The stifling heat made even talking an ordeal: it reached the point where they only talked when it was absolutely required.

Jacob's shoulder and Seth's leg gave them trouble. The pain was not severe, just nagging, and it left them very touchy. Brigham and Nancy realised this and wisely left the pair to their silences.

On the fourth day, around mid-morning, Brigham called a halt. He indicated that he didn't want anyone to speak.

The other three watched in silence as Brigham rode back part of the the way they had come. He drew rein just below a ridge, dismounted, and made his way on foot to the crest of the ridge. He spent only a few moments gazing over the ridge's crest before returning to his horse and riding back to join them.

'How far off are they?' Seth asked.

There was no need for any of them to

ask who was beyond the ridge. They all knew, for they had all been waiting for this moment since they had ridden out of Youngtown; they had all been waiting for it to happen, yet all of them had been hoping that it never would.

Brigham tipped his dusty hat to the back of his head. 'Two — maybe three hours.'

'They must have been doing some hard riding,' Seth said.

'Eager to catch a bellyful of lead,' Jacob said bitterly. He jerked his horse's head around and spurred the animal away fiercely.

Nancy exchanged worried glances with Seth and Brigham. 'He's so tired he doesn't know what he's saying,' she said, though inwardly she knew what both Seth and Brigham also knew — that Jacob was reaching the end of his patience. He was close to letting go, close to the moment when he would say to hell with law and everything else. If that happened Jacob would be deaf to all words, no matter who spoke them.

He would think only of killing before he was killed.

Watching Nancy ride after Jacob, Brigham said, 'We're going to have trouble, Seth. I can see it coming.'

'Let's hope we get to Blanco Station before Retford reaches us,' Seth answered.

'No disrespect, Seth, but your badge didn't stop Retford. You think LeRoy's will do any better?'

'That drowning man who grabs a handful of straw doesn't stop to figure whether or not they'll do him any good,' Seth said. 'Brig, he just grabs.'

Seth's words were still being tossed around in Brigham's mind late in the afternoon of the next day when they rode into Blanco Station. They'd ridden all night and all the day, and they had gained some three hours on the Retford bunch who had pushed their horses too hard for too long.

The station was little more than a sprawling log and adobe cabin, corral and stable, along with a couple of outhouses. Before the station ran the shallow stream that gave the place its name — Blanco Creek. The Creek originated high up in the San Juan Mountains, flowing down to the lowlands in the north, then curving off to the east to eventually join up with the Rio Grande just below Arroyo Hondo.

As they rode through the creek and up the dusty slope that fronted the station a door opened in the cabin. Two men stepped out; one moved out into the yard, the other stayed close by the cabin wall.

Noting the burnished badge on the shirt of the man who had stepped forward, Seth drew rein before him.

'I'm Seth Tyler,' he offered.

The other nodded. He was a tall man, with a strong-boned face. Dark eyes studied Seth closely. 'LeRoy,' he said finally. 'I hear you've had some hard times up in Hope.'

'It's a hard place, but it's coming along. It'll take some taming. I don't expect it to come easy.'

LeRoy glanced beyond Seth. His gaze settled on Jacob. 'You the one all this fuss is about?' he asked.

'Depends which way you look at it,' Jacob said testily.

'Don't you give me trouble, boy,' LeRoy snapped.

'Don't give me cause,' Jacob threw back.

Seth turned his horse sharply. 'Jacob, ease off. Just sit calm.'

But Jacob wasn't listening. His attention had been drawn to the man who had been standing in the shadow of the cabin wall. Now the man had moved forward into the open. He was slender, pale-faced, with blonde hair and very pale eyes. His hands were slim, womanlike, the fingers long.

'Seth, what the hell is this?' Jacob asked suddenly. 'What's he doing here?'

LeRoy inclined his head towards the man who had moved to stand at his side. 'Boone is with me,' he stated.

'With you?' Jacob repeated, anger rising in his voice.

'As I said, Boone is with me. He's my deputy.'

'Goddamn it, Seth, you said they were sending help from Amarillo. Hell, you didn't say anything about the kind of man they were taking on these days. Must be easy to get a badge these days. All you have to be is a lowdown, yellow-bellied backshooter like Virgil Boone.'

Nancy had moved in beside Brigham and she was the only one who heard him speak, though it was more to himself than to anyone around him, and she didn't understand what he meant anyway.

'Hell, Seth,' Brigham sighed, 'they went and set fire to that straw we grabbed ahold of.'

14

Alvin LeRoy followed Seth towards the corral. He watched silently while Seth put the wary animals into the enclosure, unsaddled and fed them, brought them water.

'What's this trouble between your brother and my deputy?' LeRoy asked eventually. 'I want to know, Tyler. I can't have friction lousing up the works when the Retfords get here.'

Seth closed the corral. He wiped sweat from his face. 'Goes back to the War,' he said. 'Something that happened between Jacob and Virgil Boone at the Battle of Shiloh. Jacob swears that Boone caused the death of six men through his own cowardice. They'd always had bad blood between them. Ever since Boone joined our unit. All we know is that six men did die. There were no witnesses. Just Jacob and

Boone. After it happened we had to spend most of our time keeping them apart. If we'd let them they would have killed each other.'

'If you don't mind me saying so, Tyler, your brother seems to have a natural instinct for getting into trouble.'

Seth turned sharply, his face angry. 'You hinting that maybe Jacob started all this mess with the Retfords? Maybe you think he's gun-happy? Kill-crazy or something?'

'I ain't hinting anything. Just making an observation is all.'

Seth walked slowly back towards the cabin. The others were all inside, save for Virgil Boone. He was leaning against the cabin wall, a long thin cigar between his narrow lips. As Seth approached he eased away from the wall. There was a faint smile on his face. His coat was pulled back to show the short-barrelled Colt that was worn low in a plain, black holster. There was something in the way he wore it that said it was there for much more than just show.

'I'd walk easy with LeRoy,' Boone said softly. 'He's got a reputation that marks him as a real hard hombre. Get on his wrong side and you'll wish you'd stayed out there with the Retfords.'

'You think that badge he wears is big enough to hide you as well as that yellow-streak you carry?'

Boone's face turned ashen, then burned fiercely with anger. 'Now look, Tyler, no two-bit town lawman's going to talk to me like that.'

'You going to do something about it, Boone? Like maybe shoot me in the back?' Seth tipped his stained hat to the back of his head. 'You weren't man enough to carry those sergeants stripes back at Shiloh. I don't figure a U.S. marshal's badge is going to make much difference.'

Boone took a hard step forward. For a moment Seth thought he'd pushed Boone too far. The deputy's right hand was hovering over the smooth-worn butt of his Colt. A muscle trembled tautly in the drawn, pale skin of his left cheek.

'Boone!'

LeRoy's voice was a harsh whipcrack against the still silence. He was still standing by the corral.

'Over here, Boone, I want you now.' It was an order, not a request, and it worked like a release spring on Virgil Boone's taut nerves. He relaxed visibly, his breath coming from him slowly as he straightened up.

'Scoot, boy, the bossman's calling,' Seth said.

Boone bit down hard on his cigar and stepped around Seth, made his way across to where LeRoy stood.

Seth watched him for a moment, then turned and opened the cabin door and went inside.

As Seth entered the cabin Jacob glanced up from the mug of coffee he was nursing. There was still anger close to the surface and it showed in Jacob's set face. The sudden confrontation with Virgil Boone had been bad for Jacob. The way things were right now, Virgil Boone was one man Jacob could do without. One patch of trouble was enough to clear up at one time.

Jacob swallowed a mouthful of hot coffee. He'd laced it with sugar but it still tasted bitter. He put the mug down and pushed it away from him.

'Don't let it bother you, Jacob.'

Jacob glanced up and smiled at Nancy. 'I'm trying. Trouble is I just keep thinking how many people are getting involved in my troubles.'

'You mean me? Seth? Brigham?' Nancy sat down beside him. 'Only because we want to. Because your troubles are ours. Surely you know that.'

'Maybe. LeRoy's not too sure.'

'He's working by the rulebook. He must see that this trouble isn't of your making.'

'And Boone?'

'Is it so bad between you, Jacob?'

He gave her a wry smile. 'If you knew,' he said gently.

The station manager came through from the kitchen then.

'Food's ready,' he said.

15

Darkness came swiftly, bringing with it the sudden chill of the desert country. Bright stars shone down from the vaulted sweep of the deep sky.

There had been no sign of the Retfords during the daylight hours. They were close by, but keeping out of sight. Only Jacob knew they were out there in the darkness, biding their time, waiting for the right moment.

It was close on midnight when it happened.

At first there was only the darkness beyond the soft glow thrown by the lamps of the way station. And then as if someone had opened a door the night was lighted up by the muzzle-flashes of a dozen guns and the silence was shattered by the crackling roar of exploding cartridges. Heavy bullets slammed into the cabin walls. Some came in through the open windows. A lamp burst into sudden flame as a bullet struck it and the oil ignited. Brig grabbed up a blanket and swiftly doused the flames.

The shooting lasted for a couple of minutes. Then it stopped as abruptly as it had started. Silence came again, deep and dark.

In the shadowed gloom of the cabin someone moved. Broken glass shattered underfoot.

'You still figure to have a polite talk with the Retfords, Mister LeRoy?' Jacob's voice was deliberately measured. He felt a brief satisfaction at LeRoy's discomfort.

'You ain't in the clear yet, boy,' LeRoy said in clipped tones.

Jacob sat back on his heels in the darkness. Nancy was beside him. She was silent, but he felt the tension that gripped her and he reached out a big hand to her, felt her own touch it and grip it.

'We'll make it, Jacob,' he heard her whisper.

I hope so, Jacob said silently to himself.

They kept a constant watch throughout the night, but there was no more from the Retfords. Jacob himself was at one of the windows as dawn broke. He watched with tired eyes as the sun rose and flooded the land with rosy light.

Just before full light Brigham and Seth slipped outside and brought the horses round to the rear of the cabin. They saddled them up and loose-tied them.

Coffee was ready when they got back inside. Seth brought a mug over to Jacob.

'Ease off, Jacob,' he said. 'We'll get this settled one way or another today.'

Jacob took a deep swallow of the hot brew. 'Amen.'

The long black shadows of the dawn were still fading when a line of men appeared over a low ridge just beyond the corral. They were on foot. Jacob counted eleven of them. He turned from the window.

'LeRoy, you feel like talking?'

LeRoy went to the window and looked out. 'Which is Kyle?'

'The big one in the black shirt,' Jacob said.

LeRoy turned away from the window. 'Boone, you stay in here. I don't want Tyler out there under any circumstances.' He glanced at Jacob. 'You hear?'

Jacob opened his mouth to speak, but Seth stepped forward. 'He'll stay.'

LeRoy glanced again at Jacob, his eyes almost asking Jacob to argue, but Jacob had recognised the no-nonsense tone of Seth's voice and remained silent.

Moving over to the window Jacob looked out. The Retford bunch had gathered just beyond the corral. They seemed to be waiting for something to happen. Watching them Jacob suddenly felt tired of the whole damned affair. Despite the fact that he didn't particularly like LeRoy, he hoped that the man could bring an end to the mess. Jacob realised that all he wanted to do was to just ride out with his brothers and Nancy. He thought of Virgil Boone, the memory of that bloody day of death and treachery back at Shiloh, and even that failed to anger him as it had only a few hours back.

He heard the cabin door open and from his window he saw LeRoy step out into the early sunlight. Seth followed him. Both men carried rifles, both had their holstered guns clear. Jacob watched them as they began the long walk across the open yard.

Jacob levered a round into the breech of his rifle and rested it across the sill of the window.

'Keep your finger off that trigger, Tyler,' Virgil Boone's voice came from close behind Jacob.

Jacob turned his head. 'Boone, you back off, and fast. My brother is out there and I'm not giving anybody the chance to cold-deck him.'

'You do as I say,' Boone said. His face was dark with anger.

From across the room Brigham's voice reached them. 'Jacob, you just carry on with what you're doing. Boone ain't going to bother you. I got me a cocked .44–40 pointing at him that'll guarantee it.'

Boone spun round, his finger pointing at Brigham. 'I can have you arrested for this,' he yelled. 'Preventing an appointed U.S. lawman from doing his duty.'

'Why, Boone, I'm not preventing you from doing anything. Just letting you know I'm going to shoot you if you do it.'

Before anyone could speak or move there came the sound of a shot from outside. Jacob turned back to the window in time to see Kyle Retford fall, a bright patch of blood staining the black shirt over his heart. In the same instant Seth took a quick step forward and laid his rifle-barrel across the skull of one of Retford's men. The man went down on his knees, his handgun slipping from his fingers. Then Seth and

LeRoy were advancing on the rest of Retford's bunch who were milling about in an uncertain mass, leaderless and not too eager to get involved with the law.

Nancy joined Jacob at the window. She suddenly said, 'Where's Will? Will Retford. Jacob, he should be with them.'

Brigham had just left the cabin, making his way over to help Seth and LeRoy. Boone was standing in the centre of the floor looking out through the open door.

From out at the back of the cabin a horse snorted, as if disturbed. Jacob raised his head. Will Retford.

'Out back,' he said to Nancy. He put his rifle down, drew his handgun and started for the cabin's rear door.

'Hey!' Boone's hand shot out, caught Jacob's sleeve, pulling him round in a half circle. Without hesitation Jacob drove his left fist out, catching Boone across the jaw. The deputy stumbled back, going down on one knee, blood streaking his mouth.

Jacob reached the rear door, put his shoulder against it and went on through as the door burst open. As he stepped outside he came face to face with Will Retford. Will was in the act of loosing the tethered horses, his hand reaching out for the tied reins, but the moment he set eyes on Jacob, recognising him, something made him back off. He turned away, as if to run, his hand clawing for his gun as he moved.

Seeing Will's hand going for his gun, Jacob launched himself in a swift leap. He slammed into Will and the pair of them sprawled full-length in the dust. There was a moment of wild thrashing as each man tried to gain the upper hand. Then Will kicked himself clear, rolling frantically as he tried to escape from Jacob's grasp. He got to his feet, aiming a savage kick at Jacob's face. Jacob twisted his body to one side, but the toe of Will's boot caught his shoulder. Pain engulfed his shoulder. Rolling in under Will's boot Jacob pushed himself upright, smashing heavily into Will. Will gave a yell as he was knocked off his feet. He slammed hard down into the dust, and before he could move Jacob was standing over him. There was a moment of complete stillness, and then Jacob reached down with his left hand and grabbed Will's collar, yanking him to his feet.

As Jacob lifted Will upright, Virgil Boone burst out of the cabin. His hair was streaked across his face and he had smeared the blood on his mouth with the back of his hand. He ran out into the open and stopped, his hand going for his holstered gun.

'Tyler!' His voice was a high scream of anger. 'Let go of that man and throw down your gun. I aim to finish you this time, you bastard.'

As Jacob turned to face Boone he saw Nancy step out of the cabin. She took in the scene quickly, and before Jacob could speak she had stepped forward, reaching to restrain Boone's gunhand.

Boone gave a smothered oath. His arm swept up, his hand thrusting Nancy to one side.

Jacob took a swift step forward, anger darkening his face. 'Boone!' he said, his voice harsh.

As Boone glanced his way, his gunhand rising, Nancy threw herself towards him again. Her hands caught the Colt as it came clear of Boone's holster.

Jacob, still holding the struggling Will Retford, saw her situation, and he cast Will aside as he made for Nancy and Virgil Boone.

He was too late. Without warning Boone's gun exploded with a harsh roar. Nancy gave a startled cry as she was flung away from Boone's side. The smoking gun was still in her hands, her fingers tightly clutched around the barrel. She stumbled and fell to her knees.

Boone was staring down at his chest, his face ashen. He raised his head to look at Jacob, shock in his eyes. Blood was pumping out of the raw wound in his chest.

Jacob could feel his fingers gripping his gunbutt tightly. He took a step forward as he saw Nancy pushing to her feet, but then, from behind, he heard a faint sound — a sound he recognised. It was a gun-hammer being cocked. Will Retford! Jacob had almost forgotten him.

He turned, bringing up his gun as he did. Will was by his horse, which he'd left close by. He had one foot in the stirrup, and as Jacob came about, Will levelled his Colt and fired. The bullet missed Jacob, who returned the fire. His bullet cut a red gash across Will's cheek. Will gave a pained yell as he hurled himself on to his horse, yanking the reins round savagely, sending the animal crashing through the brush and out of sight.

Jacob, turning back to Nancy, saw Virgil Boone falling forward on to his face. And beyond him Jacob saw with a sudden shock, the form of Nancy, down on the ground, lying still.

He ran to her, went down on his knees beside her, and knew the moment her face came into view that there was nothing he could do for her. Nancy was dead.

A wild and burning anger swept over him as he thought of the one who had done this. Will Retford! Will's hastily fired bullet had taken Nancy's life, snatching her from Jacob and leaving him with nothing but his life, which was as empty now as the substance of his shattered dreams.

Jacob found himself remembering all that had happened since he and Nancy had come together back on that bleak mountain. He remembered how they had talked of a future together when all this trouble was over. There would be no future now — not ever.

Run fast, Will. Run fast and far, but don't ever think it's far enough. I'll follow you till I die and I'll get you. One way or another, Will, I'll get you.

Again the now too familiar sound of

a gun-hammer clicking, brought Jacob back to the cold surroundings of reality.

'You finally did it, Tyler. You just couldn't let go till you'd killed Boone!'

The voice was LeRoy's. It was hard and cold, and Jacob realised he was in a blind canyon with no way out. He saw how bad it looked for him: Nancy dead, with Boone's gun in her hands; and Boone dead too, unarmed, with himself close by, a drawn gun in his hand. LeRoy had stepped out of the cabin too late to see Will's fatal shot. Too late to see Will ride off, leaving Jacob alone. To LeRoy it was plain, clear evidence. Damning evidence in LeRoy's eyes. His rigid code of right and wrong, his knowledge of the long-standing grievance between Boone and Jacob. The odds were piling up against Jacob almost faster than he could count.

'Ease up, Tyler,' LeRoy said. 'Keep that gunhand by your side. Don't give me the excuse I need to put you down.'

Jacob stood up slowly. LeRoy was in a vicious mood, his tolerance stretched to the limit. He'd already killed one man — Kyle Retford — and it wouldn't take much to push him beyond the limit.

'Turn around. Face to me,' LeRoy said.

Jacob turned carefully. The rifle in LeRoy's hands was held straight and steady, aimed squarely at Jacob.

'No way out of this one, boy,' LeRoy said tightly. 'No smartass talk. I've got you cold, and I'll see you hang. You did wrong when you went up against that badge.'

The man was bound and determined to see him hang. The realisation hit Jacob hard. There was no way to convince LeRoy that he hadn't shot Boone. There was only one man who could do that. Will Retford! But first Jacob had to find him — and then he had to get him to confess his guilt.

His immediate concern was getting away from LeRoy. The way LeRoy was talking he would have Jacob in shackles once he got him back inside the cabin.

Jacob's chance had to be taken now, before his hands were tied, literally.

And almost as the thought crossed his mind Jacob acted. It was an instinctive move, motivated by a purely animal instinct to survive.

He threw himself forward and sideways, his action taking him away from LeRoy's rifle a second before it fired. And then Jacob's shoulder caught LeRoy just below the knees, sending the lawman stumbling back. Then LeRoy was falling, Jacob following him down, and before LeRoy could recover his balance Jacob was on him. The heavy pistol in Jacob's hand rose and fell in a continuous movement. LeRoy grunted as the barrel struck him. Blood flowed from a gash in his forehead as he sank unconscious to the ground.

Jacob got to his feet and walked away from where Nancy lay, past the sprawled form of Virgil Boone. He reached the horses and untied his own animal, checking that everything was in place. He'd picked up LeRoy's rifle and shoved it into the sheath on the saddle.

Swinging into the saddle Jacob reined the horse around in a tight circle and moved off at a fast walk. He took the horse on through the brush where Will Retford had taken his animal. The tracks were pretty clear here. Those tracks would take him to Will — after that Jacob wasn't too sure how things might work out. Will wasn't going to come back calmly with him and tell it the way it was. But one way or the other Will was going to put the story straight. No matter how long it took, or how far he had to go, Jacob was going to set it right. There was no way around it. He had to clear his name or LeRoy would brand him as a killer. Of that Jacob had no doubt. It chafed him that he hadn't been able to see Nancy put to rest properly. Brig and Seth would see to that for him, he knew, but it wasn't the right way. He would have felt better if he'd been able to tell them the way it was. But he knew they'd figure the right telling. They knew he wasn't the kind to run out when trouble came up. They'd know he had a good reason, and that he would get back to them somehow.

The station slid out of sight below a crumbling ridge and Jacob was alone. Far ahead of him, off to the southeast he could see a figure on horseback. Will was pushing his horse hard. But Jacob just settled in his saddle and followed the tracks that led off into the bleached emptiness. Come on, Will, he begged, just look round because I'm coming for you.

The sun arced higher in the sky and beat down on the wide land. It sucked up the last of the night's moisture, bleaching the dust and the rocks a little whiter. Jacob began to sweat. He felt it dampen his shirtback, and he pulled his hatbrim down to shade his eyes, hunching his shoulders against the hard hand of the sun. It was, he thought, going to be a long, hot day, and a damned hard ride.

And it was. Will Retford knew the country well, while Jacob was a stranger to it. Though he forced the pace he found himself unable to close the gap. In fact it became greater, and as darkness fell Jacob realised he'd lost Will completely. He didn't let it worry him overly. Even if he couldn't see Will himself there were still tracks to follow. Despite his impatience Jacob slowed down. He decided to make camp for the night. There was nothing to be gained by stumbling about in the dark in strange country. He didn't want to risk injury to his horse.

Jacob found a suitable place and made camp. He lit a small fire, making no attempt at concealing it. He wanted Will to know he was being followed. After a quick meal and a couple of mugs of strong, hot coffee Jacob rolled into his blanket. He intended to be up at first light. The trouble was that sleep wouldn't come. There was too much on his mind. Nancy's death, and the trouble he was in. He found himself thinking of Will Retford, of his brothers — yet over all others the strongest thoughts were of Virgil Boone. If Boone hadn't been with LeRoy the whole thing might not have happened. Jacob was sure of that. Though he hadn't thought about the man for a long time, somewhere at the back of his mind, Jacob had known that he and Virgil Boone would meet again. There had been something that had needed settling between them. In his wildest imaginings Jacob had never envisaged that meeting taking place under such complicated circumstances, or ending so tragically.

As he lay there Jacob found his mind going back in time, back to the day he first came into contact with Virgil Boone . . .

It was 1862. Jacob, along with Seth and Brig, were serving together in the same Union Army unit. The Civil War was at its height, Union and Confederate forces were constantly locked in fierce battles. It was during an infrequent lull that Virgil Boone had joined the Tylers' unit. Boone was a sergeant, and shortly after his arrival Jacob found himself assigned to a small squad under Boone's charge, given the task of taking a number of Confederate prisoners to a nearby Union stockade. It wasn't long before Boone's character began to reveal itself. He was a vicious bully who took a delight in terrorising defenceless men, and though Jacob despised Boone for it he had to tread carefully, for Boone had the support of an influential major in the regiment. This initial instance of Boone's nature was soon to show itself again, and Jacob, though still aware of the trouble he could cause for himself, was unable to stay silent for long.

He realised later that he should have confided in someone from the start. But Jacob was the kind of man who preferred to work out his own problems. He kept his thoughts to himself, not even telling Seth or Brigham; they were all fighting a war, and Jacob knew they had enough on their minds. They would have backed him if he'd spoken up, but Jacob let it be, content to observe Boone on his own.

It quickly became clear to him that Boone was an opportunist. Virgil Boone was in the War for one reason only — to further himself at whatever cost, no matter who got hurt in the process. A little quiet investigating revealed that Boone was doing a fair amount of illicit trading in army stores and supplies. Jacob found out that Boone's contact was a burly Virginian named Byard. Wherever the Regimental Supply Unit made camp, Byard showed up, in the guise of a travelling preacher. He would tour the camp, giving prayer-meetings and comfort to those who needed it — only each time he left camp his wagon carried out more than it had brought in. Jacob found out too that Boone's major, one Stavro Banacek, was also in on the dealing. This made things a little more difficult for Jacob. He was going to have to be very sure of his facts if he was contemplating accusing a major of stealing army supplies.

Before he could even think much about the matter the chance was taken from him as the brief lull in the fighting ended. The Confederate forces began to launch massive attacks and the Union Army was plunged into weeks of heavy fighting. Jacob had no time to worry about Boone in the desperate engagements that followed. Just staying alive was enough for any man.

During more than one battle Jacob noticed Boone applying his skills at avoiding exposing himself in dangerous positions. Boone used his rank to keep himself in the background as much as possible, while sending many a man forward into combat; but he managed to do it in a way that went unobserved except by Jacob, who was paying more attention to the man than anyone else. Rapidly he became more and more angered at the man's cowardice.

In the middle of one bloody encounter, on a day when the skies had opened to flood the land with rain, Jacob found himself isolated in a stand of trees along with a couple of the men from his squad — and Virgil Boone. For once Boone was forced to fight for his life and it was plain that he wasn't enjoying it. He fired at anything and everything, using a lot of ammunition but doing little good. He was continually screaming orders at Jacob and the other men, all of which boiled down to the simple directive: keep in front of me and I'll stay well to the rear!

Despite the rapid fire from the Henry rifles being used by Jacob and the others, the Confederates pushed forward. Jacob and the other men began to fall back while Virgil Boone yelled at them to hold their positions. He was ignored, and he began to panic.

A Confederate bullet killed one of Jacob's companions, and a minute later the second Union soldier went down, blood pumping from a gaping wound in his left thigh. Jacob realised that all they could do now was retreat, and fast, in the hope of getting back to the rest of their unit.

He turned to find Boone. He wanted the man's help in getting the wounded trooper out. Instead he found Boone standing over the fallen man, ordering him back to his position. The trooper, a white-faced boy, was crying in pain and terror, unmindful of Boone's ranting as he tried to stem the flow of blood that was pouring from his leg. Jacob felt his control slip, and his anger rose up in a blazing surge as he reached Boone.

'Tyler, I want you to be a witness,' Boone screamed. 'This man will not get back to his post! He had no right to fall back! You will remain here while I go back and inform Command of our situation and this soldier's disobedience!'

'I got permission to fall down if I'm shot dead?' Jacob asked.

Boone stared at him, his pale face blurred by the pouring rain. For a moment he was speechless. Then he gathered himself.

'What did you say, Tyler?'

'Nothing. Just give me a hand to pick

Taylor up and let's get the hell out of here, Boone!'

'Sergeant Boone to you, Tyler, and I give the orders here!' He peered closely at Jacob. 'What're you playing at, Tyler?'

Jacob sleeved rain out of his eyes. 'Something I should've done a long while ago, Boone, and I'm damn sorry I didn't!' As he spoke Jacob lashed out and hit Virgil Boone full in the mouth with all the strength he could muster. Boone gave a croak and staggered back. He stumbled and fell, going to his knees. He stayed there for a moment, then shoved to his feet, his hands clawing for the gun thrust into the holster on his belt. Jacob stepped in close and as Boone straightened up, he slammed the butt of his gun across Boone's gunhand. Boone screamed as the gun was driven from his fingers. Giving him no chance to recover, Jacob grabbed him by the collar and hurled him across the slippery grass. Boone landed on his face on the muddy ground.

Standing over him Jacob said: 'Now help me with this boy, Boone, or by all that's Holy, I'll put a slug in you right now, you thieving bastard! Major Banacek ain't here to hold your hand this time!'

Virgil Boone climbed to his feet in silence. He stared sullenly at Jacob, his eyes full of hate, and Jacob knew he'd said too much. He should have kept his mouth shut about his knowledge of Boone's connection with Banacek. It wouldn't take Boone long to realise that Jacob probably knew about Byard as well. It had been a bad slip on Jacob's part, but it was done now and there was no use worrying about it.

Jacob knew he'd made an enemy, and had probably put himself in danger from Boone and his companions. He accepted it as he always accepted danger, not letting it weigh him down, but always staying on guard against it.

'Let's go, Boone!' Jacob snapped, and after they'd picked up the wounded trooper, he made himself a promise to keep a watchful eye open for Boone's next move. He didn't know when it might come, or where, but he did know one thing — it would come . . .

Virgil Boone's partner in crime, Major Banacek, was killed in action a week before the battle at Shiloh. Byard, the bogus preacher was in camp when the news came in, and he was up and gone within minutes of hearing it. He was never seen again.

Boone was on his own, with the only man to point the finger at him — Jacob Tyler!

Since the incident on the field with the wounded trooper Jacob had kept a close watch for any move Boone might make. With Banacek's death Jacob saw that Boone was liable to start worrying; with the major alive Virgil Boone could breathe easy. He was under Banacek's protection. Now, with Banacek dead and Byard long gone, there was no one to look out for Boone. Jacob figured he would be safer if he kept Boone in sight whenever he could manage it. He got the feeling that Boone would try anything if he became nervous enough.

Boone chose his day well. 6 April 1862. The day of the Battle of Shiloh.

It began badly for the Union force. A surprise attack at dawn by the Confederate forces, 40,000 strong against Grant's Army near the Tennessee River. From the start the battle raged fiercely and the Union forces were slowly driven back to the river bank, where they had to hold out until the following morning when two Union gunboats came up and shelled the Confederate lines, driving them from the battlefield. By the time it was all over both sides had lost 10,000 men and the Confederate commander, Albert Johnston, was dead.

Jacob, along with Seth and Brigham fought alongside the rest of their company. After the initial attack the Union force began to spread out and fight back, finding cover wherever it could. Cavalry units found themselves on foot after their mounts were run off.

It was a back and forth battle for a while, but gradually the Union force was driven back towards the river, fighting every inch of the way.

During the morning Jacob got himself separated from Seth and Brigham. He had little time to worry about it, for the Confederates were pressing hard on the Union lines and it was fire and fire again, reload and fire again at the ranks of gray figures coming across the fields.

He found himself at one point pinned down behind a fallen tree, with a number of Confederate rifles turned his way. Jacob downed two rebels when they tried to make a run for his hiding place. After that the others left him alone and Jacob was able to crawl away from his tree into the cover of a nearby wood. He used the moment of calm to reload his gun, then began to move through the wood, making his way back towards the Union lines.

Then he came on a group of men trying to drag a cannon out of a muddy stream-bed. There were six troopers, a young officer, and Virgil Boone.

'You need some help, sir?' Jacob asked.

The young officer glanced up at Jacob and nodded. 'We do, soldier. Trying to get this cannon out of here and down to the river. There are supplies of powder and shot there for this.'

Jacob put his rifle down and put his sholder to the cannon along with the others. He sensed Virgil Boone watching him, but he ignored the man.

Slowly the combined efforts of the men brought the cannon out of the stream and on to level ground.

'All right, boys,' the officer said, 'let's get this gun rolling. See if we can send some Yankee ball over to those damned rebels!'

And right then a number of Confederates burst out of the trees behind them. A rattle of rifle fire burst out.

Jacob spun round, grabbing for his rifle. As he swung the gun around he saw the young officer crashing to the ground, a bloody wound in his chest, the back of his blue uniform torn and red. And then Jacob was firing, sending shot after shot at the running gray figures. Other rifles joined his as the six Union troopers picked up their own weapons.

The exchange lasted for only a few seconds. Four rebels went down and the few remaining ran for the cover of the dense trees.

'Let's move this damn gun,' Jacob said.

'Tyler, I'll give the orders!' Virgil Boone yelled.

'Then give 'em, 'cause we ain't staying here long,' Jacob told him.

The other men exchanged glances; obviously there was something between these two. Most of the men knew Jacob, liked him. Boone, on the other hand, wasn't popular with anyone.

'Tyler, you go against me and I'll have you court-martialled! These men will be my witnesses!'

'Damnit, Boone, to Hell with our

grievances! Let's get this cannon rolling. There's a battle going on and we need this gun. I'll face you anytime after this is over, but right now I don't give a damn about you or what you're shouting about!'

Jacob turned to the cannon and looked at the six troopers. 'Come on, boys, how about a hand?'

The six hesitated for a moment, then joined Jacob at the gun. As they got it rolling they were all too busy to notice Virgil Boone's next move.

If Jacob hadn't been where he was he too would have gone without noticing. He was, however, in the right place at the right time, and that saved his life.

He happened to glance up, wanting to know where Boone was, and he saw the man straightaway. Boone was standing behind the thick trunk of a tree, looking back into the wood, his face white with fear, his eyes staring. Sweat shone on his skin.

Jacob threw a quick glance in the direction Boone was looking, and he saw a great number of Confederates coming out of the trees. There were scores of them, too many to count, and they'd seen the cannon and the men pushing it.

In that moment Boone threw a frightened glance towards the cannon. For a scant second his eyes met Jacob's, and then, before even Jacob knew what he was up to, Boone had melted quickly to one side, easing himself into the thick brush and trees. He'd done it without being seen by the advancing Confederate force, for the tree he'd stood behind hid him from them.

Too late Jacob realised what had happened. Boone had gone, deserting his men without even warning them, taking himself off into the cover of the trees without making a sound.

In the few seconds the whole episode took, Jacob found himself the only one knowing about the rebels. He began to shout a warning and then the whole world exploded with sound as a dozen, maybe more, Confederate rifles opened up on the men around the cannon. Something caught Jacob on the back of the head and he pitched forward across the cannon, then slid to the ground. He heard more shots, men screaming. A heavy weight fell across him. He could feel something warm running down his face, and then the world went dark and silent and he knew no more.

He didn't see the six troopers cut down in a ragged volley of shots that tore their bodies into bloody rags. Nor did he see the mass of rebels sweep on by the gun and its seven minders. He lay unconscious, with one of the dead troopers lying across him. He didn't hear the battle fade into the distance, leaving the dim wood silent again until the birds came back to settle on the trees.

He came to later with a sickening headache and the back of his head sticky with blood. There was a lot of blood on his face and shirt, but that had come from the dead trooper lying across him. Jacob got himself clear and stood up. He was dizzy, sick. He hunted round for his rifle, checked it over.

He spent an unpleasant few minutes trying to find a sign of life in the bodies of the troopers, but there was nothing. They were all dead, and that made Jacob angry. None of them had had a chance. Not even to defend themselves. They hadn't been warned. Given a chance they might have fought their way out, but Virgil Boone had taken that chance from them when he'd failed to call out.

Jacob stood up, his face drawn and angry. Boone! Damn the man! Where was he? Still running for his miserable life! Someone ought to shoot him down like the dog he was. Six good men were dead because of Boone's cowardice. And Jacob counted himself lucky to be alive. Maybe he could do something about Boone now. If he'd spoken up sooner perhaps this might not have happened. But Jacob didn't reproach himself too much. No good mooning over something in the past. Maybe he should have said something, but he hadn't, and that was that.

Perhaps his chance would come. Boone would show up somewhere, sometime. And maybe then . . . what? Jacob had a feeling he was kidding himself. Boone wouldn't stand up and fight. He'd refuse to face Jacob with a gun, and no matter how much he hated the man, Jacob knew he wasn't about to shoot him down without a chance.

Jacob turned away from the place of death and moved off through the wood, heading back for the Union lines, keeping his eyes open for any sign of the enemy — and for Virgil Boone!

But his chance never came. Fate stepped in and took Boone away before Jacob could settle with him except for a couple of brief meetings, which gave Jacob the chance to land a few well-delivered blows. Seth and Brigham, who now knew the story, were forced to step in and restrain their brother. They knew how he felt, but they knew that

Jacob's fiery temper was liable to land him deep in trouble before he could explain his hatred for Boone. A week later Virgil Boone was transferred to another company, and Jacob never saw him again. Not until the day he showed up at Blanco Station with Alvin LeRoy . . .

Jacob sat up and threw his blanket aside. He reached for the pot of coffee he'd left on the fire and poured himself a mug. Damn Boone! He wished he could get the man out of his mind. He had enough problems to handle without being haunted by the man's image. He drank the bitter coffee. It was something that would fade in time. Jacob lay down again, dragging his blanket over him. His prime concern now was Will Retford. No matter how long it took. No matter how far he had to go. He had to find Will, and somehow get him to tell the truth, the way it had really happened back there at Blanco Station.

As he finally drifted off into a restless

sleep Jacob didn't realise just how far he would have to go, or the things that were waiting for him. Even if he had it wouldn't have made any difference, or stopped him!

16

By mid-afternoon the herd had settled in the stockpens at the north end of Bannock, and a couple of hours later Dunhill had collected his money and paid off the crew.

Standing on the boardwalk outside the cattle-company office, Jacob Tyler stared hard at the roll of bills in his hand. It had been some long time since he'd held such an amount. It had been more or less this way since that day back at Blanco Station; the day when Virgil Boone and Nancy had died, and Jacob had taken off after Will Retford. He'd lost count of the long months that had slid by, had long since stopped counting the miles as he trailed Will. Jacob had expected a long chase, but by no means as long as this. Will Retford had proved to be a damn sight smarter than Jacob had at first anticipated. It soon became apparent that Will knew a lot of country very well; he seemed to know a thousand places to hide, and he also seemed to have a lot of friends. More than once Jacob had met hostility when he'd asked questions about Will. But Jacob knew he had to keep looking. Will was his only proof that he hadn't killed Virgil Boone, and Jacob knew he was going to have to have that proof before he could determine his innocence to the one man who seemed bound to try and get him hanged — U.S. Marshall Alvin LeRoy. LeRoy was on his trail most of the time; the marshal had other duties, but his prime target, almost his obsession, was Jacob, and whenever their paths happened to come close to crossing, LeRoy made it his business to go after Jacob; more than once Jacob had come close to falling foul of LeRoy, but his instinct for survival somehow managed to keep him free.

When his money ran out Jacob was forced to abandon his pursuit of Will

Retford. He took any job that came his way, not that he found it difficult; Jacob was a good man with cattle and there was plenty of work in that line; he took other jobs too, not always to his taste, but Jacob knew that to continue his chase after Will he had to eat and survive the cold winter, to keep himself in clothing and ammunition. So he worked as he followed Will, taking himself through the long winter, picking up information as he went, until now, in late spring he found himself at the end of a two month cattle-drive that had brought him to this remote little town called Bannock, high up in the wild Teton country of Wyoming.

It wasn't much of a town either. Just a single street, rutted and spongy with spring rain. The town had survived a long, hard winter, and it showed; the buildings were all ready for a coat of paint and from what Jacob had seen of the citizens of Bannock they might have benefited from a little brightening up themselves.

Jacob folded his money and put it away in his shirt pocket. He squared his hat and stared up and down the street until he spotted what he was looking for. A shave and a hot bath were priorities on Jacob's list, then a change of clothing. And after that a good meal.

On his way down to the barber-shop Jacob passed Bannock's only saloon; from inside he could hear the celebrating of his former trail-partners; as soon as the rest of the crew had received their pay they'd headed straight for the saloon and its liquid delights, intent on some hard drinking before they rode out.

They were still making their noise when Jacob came out of the barber-shop close on an hour later.

He passed on down the street, pushing his way into a crowded restaurant where he ordered beefsteak and fried potatoes, beans and a pot of coffee.

While he ate Jacob reviewed his position: he had money now, enough to keep him in supplies for a good few months: before him lay the prospect of more searching for Will, all the time watching over his shoulder for sign of LeRoy: the thought of it all did little to help Jacob's peace of mind, but he knew he had no choice.

He finished his meal and left the restaurant, wandering out on to the boardwalk. He stood for a time watching the town go about its business. Somewhere, here in Bannock, Will had left a trail that Jacob needed to pick up. And once again by the time Jacob had picked up that trail, Will would be long gone. To Jacob it sometimes seemed a hell of a way to spend time.

But he knew just as well that until he had this matter settled he would never be able to find a place where he could set himself down to stay. Only when he'd cleared himself could he consider his future.

Jacob turned abruptly, angry at his morbid thoughts. He headed down the street, making for the livery where he'd stabled his horse. Before he did anything else he wanted to make sure the animal was settled. He was never sure just when he might need the speed and stamina of the powerful chestnut.

The livery was at the far end of town, standing on its own close by a cluster of corrals. As Jacob reached the open doors of the livery he became aware of the silence and emptiness that surrounded the place. Straight-away Jacob reacted, and it was without conscious thought or effort. His right hand went to the holstered colt on his right hip, easing it free in one fluid movement. But despite his speed Jacob was too late. He caught a glimpse of a lunging shadow coming in from his left, sensed more movement behind him. He half-turned, then felt a crashing blow across the side of his head. Jacob stumbled to his knees, trying to keep himself from slipping into the darkness that seemed to be engulfing him. His senses wavered, though he was still aware when rough hands grasped him, dragging him upright. A hard fist caught him in the mouth and Jacob tasted blood. He struggled against the hands that held him, but he was still weak from the blow to his head. Again and again the unseen fist delivered heavy blows to Jacob's face and body until he lost consciousness. For a moment they held him, then released him, letting Jacob slump to the ground.

He came out of the darkness slowly, feeling the pain that engulfed his body. Even before full awareness returned, Jacob realised that he was no longer in the livery. He was, he found when he finally opened his eyes, lying on a low cot. He also realised something else, and realised it very quickly — the cot he was lying on was behind bars. There was no mistaking that. Jacob sat up, swearing silently to himself as sickness rose up in him. He remained motionless for a while, waiting for the giddiness to subside.

Jacob stood up. He noticed that his gunbelt was gone from around his waist. Yet he could feel the folded wad of money still in his shirt pocket. He crossed the floor of the cell and stood at the barred door, looking out at the small, shadowed office. A desk stood over in the far corner, a man seated behind it. As Jacob reached the cell door, the man looked up. Jacob couldn't see his face. It was in deep shadow until the man stood up and walked around the desk, coming up to stand in front of the cell.

The sickness inside Jacob ceased to exist. He even forgot about the pounding driving at him from inside his skull. Everything faded from Jacob's mind as he stared at the man before him. A man wearing a gun and a town marshal's badge. A man with a face Jacob knew.

And a name Jacob knew — Will Retford!

Time had altered Will's appearance.

He was heavier now and he'd grown a thick moustache, but Jacob recognised him. And with that recognition came sudden anger. Jacob gripped the bars of the cell door until his fingers ached.

'This is the way I figured we'd meet, Tyler,' Will said, self-satisfaction in his voice.

'Just don't make the mistake of getting on the wrong side of these bars,' Jacob said softly.

Will grinned. 'Ain't no chance of that. But I aim to settle with you, Tyler, and the time's comin' fast.'

'Meaning?'

'Meaning you've gone and walked right in on a cosy set-up I got runnin' in this town. And I got to get rid of you.'

'Bullet in the back down a dark alley is more like your style.'

'I got something like that figured out.' Will reached into his shirt pocket and drew out a folded sheet of paper. He opened the paper and handed it to Jacob.

Jacob found himself looking at a poster which read: Wanted For Murder & Armed Robbery. Jacob Tyler, Formerly Of Colorado & Texas. This Man Is A Violent & Dangerous Killer. Anyone Capturing Or Aiding In The Capture Of This Fugitive Will Receive A Reward Of Five Thousand Dollars. For Information Refer To William Ford, Marshal, Bannock, Wyoming. And beneath the text was an artist's impression of Jacob's likeness.

'What the hell is this, Retford?' Jacob asked, his face angry.

'Just what it says. Round these parts you're a wanted man.' Will leaned against the wall, rolling a cigarette. 'In the last few months you and your gang have had quite a spree. Robbing banks, holding up the stages. Even a couple of railroad holdups. Killed a fair number of folks too. Only you ain't been that careful, Tyler, 'cause you got yourself recognised on one of your raids. Eye-witness!'

'Bought and paid for?'

'I don't know what you mean,' Will said.

'But I'm beginning to figure it,' Jacob said. 'Looks like you've got it made. Get yourself made marshal. Round yourself up a bunch of hardcases and start pulling robberies under the cover of the law. Smart idea. Brilliant coming from you.'

'Don't get smart, Tyler. You ain't in any position to talk clever. Mister, because of me you're a wanted man round here. Worth five thousand to any man able to pull a gun and trigger it. Just remember that. I made the frame to fit you, Tyler, and I could shoot you now and get away with it.'

'So why don't you?'

'It'll look better if you're shot while escaping. Sort of round things off nice. In a way it'll be a shame. With you dead I'll have to figure some other way of diverting attention from me and my boys. See, Tyler, you coming to Bannock has sort of spoilt my plan. But I knew sooner or later you'd turn up.

And when those boys down at the livery recognised you and jumped you, I had to jail you to keep things looking right. Being marshal I have to obey the law all the way down the line.'

'How the hell did you get that badge, Retford?'

Will touched the badge on his shirt. 'Seems I rode in at the right time. Regular marshal had just upped and died of old age. Day I arrived I got mixed up in a crooked poker game and ended up shooting the town's black sheep. Next thing I knew I was being offered the marshal's job. Seemed like a good chance so I upped and took it. Ain't looked back since.'

Behind Will the jail door opened and three men came in. They were all hard-looking individuals, wearing guns that had seen a lot of use. They sauntered across and stood looking through the bars at Jacob. Now that they were close Jacob could see that each man wore a deputy marshal's badge.

'Like you to meet some of my boys,' Will said. 'Bodrey. Kilter. Jackson.'

'So this is the feller been giving us all the trouble?' Kilter said.

'Robbin' banks and the like,' Bodrey added.

Jackson smiled coldly. 'Territory'll be a safer place with him out of the way.'

'Bright bunch you've hired yourself,' Jacob said to Will.

'Don't let 'em fool you, Tyler. These boys could take you without losin' breath.'

'Three against one unarmed man? You figure they could manage?' Jacob was letting himself become restless and roused, and when he got that way he had a tendency to use words recklessly.

'You got a loose mouth, pilgrim,' Jackson said; he was a tall man, wide at the shoulders. His arms were long, his hands large and thick-fingered. 'I figure maybe I'll have to tighten it up some.'

'Ease off,' Will said. 'You might get your chance, but not now. I want you to round up Link and Thatcher. Have them join us over at the Union. We got some business to discuss.'

'Who you going to frame for this one, Retford?' Jacob asked softly as Will's men left the jail.

Will glanced at him coldly for a moment. 'I'll figure something,' he said. 'I've got plenty of time. You haven't.'

With Will gone Jacob took stock of his situation. His position was pretty dicey. He was walking a thin line — on one side was Will and his gunhawks, on the other was the township of Bannock; to both he was a walking target, and Jacob found he was taking a dislike to both halves of the coin; whichever way it fell he was in trouble.

Jacob wandered round his small cell. It didn't take him long to realise that the only way out of the cell was by the door; Bannock's jail had been built to last and to keep its prisoners in. He stood for a time gazing at the door of the cell; like the rest of the place it was solidly constructed — it would take nothing more or less than the key to open that door, Jacob decided, and that left him right where he'd started from.

Jacob was still dwelling on the problem when the jail door opened. He looked up and saw a dark-haired young woman carrying a tray. Jacob found himself watching her closely, his attention drawn to her as she approached his cell; she was darkly attractive, her strong body moving lithely beneath the faded, taut-fitting dress and he judged her to be around twenty-three or four.

'Marshal said you'd likely be hungry,' she said, sliding the tray under the cell door.

As Jacob picked up the tray he found that the girl was watching him intently, her eyes never leaving his face. For some reason she seemed unable to look away from him. She seemed on the point of speaking again, but no words came.

'I thank you for the food, ma'am,' Jacob said.

She didn't seem to have heard him at first, but suddenly she shifted her gaze.

'You're Jacob Tyler?' Jacob nodded in answer, and the girl said 'Marshal said to stay away from you. He must figure you to be a desperate man.'

'That's his story, ma'am, but I could tell it different.'

'You don't look as black as that poster paints you.'

'No, ma'am,' Jacob said.

'Sounds like you're saying you didn't do those things.'

'I'm a stranger in this part of the country, so it's just my word.'

'Against Will Ford's?' the girl said. 'That's a greasy card you've been dealt, mister.'

Before either of them could speak again the jail door opened and the man named Jackson came in. He looked surprised when he saw the girl, and Jacob got the impression that Jackson had been expecting the jail to be deserted save for Jacob. For a moment Jackson's eyes roved freely over the girl's body, and then he strode across the floor and stood before her.

'Takin' you a time to deliver a tray of food, ain't it?'

'I figured to wait until he'd finished so I could take back the tray,' the girl said, in no way intimidated by Jackson's menace.

'So get the hell out of here! The tray can wait. Now move your ass!'

'Jackson, you need to learn manners when you talk to a lady,' Jacob said, his anger rising quickly.

A harsh laugh bubbled up out of Jackson's throat. 'Her a lady? That takes the shit! This bitch ain't no lady . . . '

The girl spun round on Jackson, so fast that he was taken off guard as her right hand swept up and caught him across the side of the face, the force of the slap knocking him against the bars of the cell.

Jacob hadn't been expecting the girl's move, but as Jackson slammed up against the bars he acted instantly, reaching through the bars to grab Jackson. One arm went around the deputy's throat, while Jacob's other hand reached for the gun holstered on the man's hip. Slipping the gun free Jacob jammed the muzzle into Jackson's side, dogging back the hammer in the same moment.

'Deputy,' Jacob said, 'you so much as breath wrong I'm liable to open a big hole in you. And don't think I won't. You got me set up as a killer, so I might as well earn the price of the reward on that poster.'

Jackson was a hard man, tough, but he wasn't stupid; he knew what a .44 calibre bullet would do to him if it was fired at this range. So he stayed very still and did exactly what Jacob told him to do.

'I figure you came back here expecting me to be on my own,' Jacob said. 'Time for me to make my break? With you close behind carrying a loaded gun?'

'Mister, I don't know what you're talking about. You crazy or something?'

Jacob gave the gun a thrust, the hard muzzle digging into Jackson's side. 'No,

I ain't crazy. Just itching to stay alive, and I wouldn't manage that for long if it was left up to you.'

Jackson began to protest then thought better of it and fell silent.

'Ma'am,' Jacob said, 'I'd be obliged if you'd leave now. I don't want to get you involved in what might happen. The minute I step out on to the street I'm going to be a target, and I wouldn't like to bring you into trouble like that.'

The girl faced Jacob squarely, her eyes fixed on him. Jacob thought he saw a gleam of tears in her eyes. He thought she was going to object.

'All right. But be careful. Will Ford is a hard man, not one I'd trust, and the men who work for him are just as bad.' She turned to go, then suddenly said: 'Take care, Jacob Tyler. I want to see you again, and I want you to be alive!'

She went then, closing the door of the jail behind her, leaving Jacob wondering about her, and despite his situation finding it hard to erase her from his mind; he found too that he wanted to see her again; in a fleeting moment of thought he realised that he didn't even know her name.

Jacob pulled himself back to the matter in hand. He still had to get out of his cell. He wasn't going to get very far while he was still behind bars.

'Deputy, I'm going to ask you a question. And you'd better give me the right answer first time. The keys to this cell. They around here?' To emphasise his point Jacob poked Jackson's side again, hard, and drew a gasp from the man.

'In the desk,' Jackson said.

'I'm going to let you go,' Jacob told him. 'And you're going to walk over to that desk, bring the keys over here and open this cell. This gun's going to be on you all the way. You want to chance trying for the door, you go ahead, but I'll tell you now I'm a fair shot.'

Jackson stepped away from the cell when Jacob released him. He half-turned his eyes moving from Jacob's face to the muzzle of the gun in Jacob's hand; watching him Jacob could almost read his thoughts: Jackson was considering the possibility of making a break.

'You wouldn't make it,' Jacob told him gently, and Jackson glared at him.

Jacob watched the deputy cross the jail, go round the desk and reach into a drawer. When Jackson straightened up again he was holding a bunch of keys in his fist.

'Move it, mister, I don't figure to be in here when the rest of your bunch walks in.'

Jackson crossed over to the cell and selected a key. Without a word he unlocked the cell. Jacob motioned him inside, then stepped out of the cell, closing and locking the door.

'You won't get beyond the end of town,' Jackson said. 'Mister, you're a marked man!'

'Be surprised what I can manage,' Jacob said. He'd found his gunbelt hanging on a hook behind the desk. Strapping it on he checked the gun's ammunition.

He opened the jail door and glanced up and down the street. Bannock seemed to be going about its business normally. Jacob didn't let the fact lull him into any sense of security; he was getting the feeling that Jackson's visit to the jail had been more than just a casual affair. Jacob's mind was working along the lines that somewhere out there Will and his bunch were waiting for him to show his face. Jacob had already noticed that the jail had no back door, or windows. There was only one way in and one way out — through the door leading out on to Bannock's main street.

Jacob stayed where he was. No sense stepping out into a trap until he'd worked out whether he could do it without getting hurt; the more he thought about it, his conviction grew that Will had set up an ambush. Once Jacob showed his face outside he could be shot down as an escaped prisoner. It would get Jacob out of Will's hair, leaving him free to carry on his corrupt office in the knowledge that he didn't need to keep looking over his shoulder any longer.

The hell of it was that Jacob had just walked into it. He'd come to Bannock expecting Will to be long gone, but it hadn't been so, and Will had been more than ready for him.

Jacob quit thinking about what had happened — his problem was with the present and the fix he was in right now. Sitting down doing nothing wasn't going to get him out of it. Sooner or later Will was going to get curious as to why Jacob hadn't come out of the jail, and also why Jackson hadn't shown his face. When that did happen Jacob was going to have to move; his chances of getting away would be a lot slimmer too. So the sooner he moved the better; being a man of action rather than deep thought, Jacob reached this conclusion quickly and acted upon it straightaway.

He threw the jail open and went out on to the boardwalk in a rush, keeping low as he hugged the jail wall. Jacob's thoughts ran ahead of him, his eyes taking in the lay of the land around him. Close by was the end of the jail wall, leaving a narrow alley between it and the building next to it; here was a chance for Jacob to get off the street; once in the alley he'd have a short time under cover, and it might just give him vital seconds of time that he needed.

He was approaching the alley when the shooting started; more than one gun, coming from a distance, but they were all aimed in his direction. Jacob heard more than one bullet howl off the wall of the jail above his head. Another tore a chunk out of the boardwalk at his feet. And then, just as he cleared the edge of the boardwalk, his body turning towards the alley, Jacob felt the slamming impact of a bullet as it ripped into his left shoulder; the impact knocked Jacob to the ground. He ignored the blossoming pain, the numbness that enveloped his shoulder, and shoved to his feet. He heard shouting behind him and knew they were coming after him. On weak legs Jacob ran for the shadows of the alley. He cursed the luck that had let that bullet find him, but at least he was still able to move.

He ran into the alley, stumbling as he started in, and the movement saved his life as a gun roared from somewhere up the alley. Jacob heard the whine of the bullet as it passed over his head. Without conscious effort or thought, Jacob brought up his Colt, aiming quickly at the figure ahead of him; the Colt fired and Jacob saw the figure fall away from him. When he reached the crumpled figure Jacob found himself looking at a strange face, but the man wore a deputy's badge and the gun he still held in his hand had a faint whisp of powdersmoke issuing from the muzzle; Jacob noticed that his bullet had caught the man in his upper-thigh, there was a lot of blood and mess, but the wound wasn't fatal.

Reaching the end of the alley Jacob turned right and found himself running along the rear-lots of Bannock. To where though? His horse was still in the livery, and Jacob suddenly realised that he was heading in that direction, though he doubted if he'd make it; his whole left side down to the waist felt numb and he could feel blood coursing hotly down his body; before he could run far he was going to have to do something about his shoulder. But what?

Behind him he could hear the noise of his pursuers. Jacob knew well enough that he couldn't outrun them for very long. He paused behind a weather-beaten outhouse, turning to face his enemies and saw them moving slowly along the rear of Bannock's main street; they were all armed, yet they all moved with caution; they'd probably seen the one that Jacob had shot and they were taking care that it didn't happen to any of them.

With only seconds at his disposal Jacob looked around desperately for some way of escape, yet he saw nothing that held promise. To one side of him lay the alleys leading back on to the street, in front of him were Will's deputies, behind him lay little else, with always the chance of someone coming at him from one of the alleys. To Jacob's way of thinking the only way out seemed the thick brush that lay on his right; here, where Bannock finished, and the country took over, perhaps lay his way out. Beyond the thick, tangled brush lay the rugged, forested land of the Teton country; Jacob knew that it was hard country for a man on foot, and more so to a hurt and hunted man, but he was in no position to be choosey.

His mind made up, Jacob turned aside from the shelter of the outhouse and plunged into the heavy brush. Behind him he heard a shout; he'd been spotted. He ignored the shouts, the sudden outburst of firing that sent bullets ripping through the undergrowth around him. Jacob pushed on, running when he could, putting up with the lashing branches that cut his face.

More than once he fell and it would have been so easy to stay down, to let the tiredness overpower him, but Jacob didn't give in easy, and it wasn't in him to quit while there was still a chance.

He lost track of time. The wooded country seemed to stretch away in every direction. So Jacob just kept moving, keeping on his feet out of pure instinct; he was fighting to survive, and the thought alone kept him upright.

And finally he stopped. Exhausted, his body trembling from the effort he'd put it to. Jacob leaned against a fallen tree, his eyes searching the terrain. He saw nothing, heard nothing. But Jacob knew that somewhere Will's bunch would be looking for him. He didn't know how far he'd come. A good distance, but still not far enough when those chasing him had horses.

So where to now? Jacob wasn't sure. He glanced up into the sky and saw that it was darkening. Soon it would be dark. He'd have a better chance then. There was only one way he could go.

That was back to Bannock. Jacob needed food and treatment for his arm. He didn't fool himself. The time would come when his body would give in to its needs, no matter how much Jacob wanted to carry on. And if that happened he would have little resistance if Will's boys caught up with him. No, he told himself, there's only one thing to do — go back to Bannock and try to find that girl. He cursed himself for not having found out her name. It was going to make it harder to find her. All he had to rely on was the fact that she worked in or ran a restaurant; it seemed logical after the conversation he'd had with her and the things said while she'd been in the jail.

Jacob found himself a place where he could hide until it was full dark. He slid down into a hollow, a shadowed place overgrown with brush and grass. It was a relief to be able to relax, even if it was an alert kind of relaxation. Despite his wanting to remain aware of his surroundings, Jacob found himself slipping into a half-asleep state; he knew it was brought on mainly through his loss of blood; strangely now his shoulder didn't pain him as much; the initial pain had faded to an angry ache that nagged persistently. Jacob hardly knew it when he finally slipped into a restless sleep, his tired body winning over his trying to stay awake.

17

With one thought hammering away inside his skull, Jacob came awake suddenly. He ignored the pain in his shoulder, the weakness that made his body leaden, because the thought left him in a cold sweat.

The girl! She'd been in the jail when Jackson had come into the place, and from what had been said in the short time before she left, it didn't take too smart a man to figure out that she had a pretty good idea what was going on. It was a fair guess that Jackson would have told Will what had happened in the jail, and Will would realise that there was a witness who might speak up and say the right things to the right people; Will would have been figuring that with Jacob out of the way he was pretty well in the clear, but now there would be the girl. Jacob had no illusions over the fact that if Will considered the girl a threat he would have her dealt with.

Jacob struggled to his feet. He stood for a moment, his senses reeling. He felt sick, his strength drained away. Despite this Jacob set off towards Bannock. He had to reach the girl and warn her she was in danger. He knew that already he could be too late; Will might have made his move, and though the thought hurt, Jacob was forced to admit that the girl might be dead. He hoped not. Still in his mind was that first meeting; he recalled the looks the girl had given him and the need in himself to see her again, and in recalling that Jacob realised he wanted to see that girl badly — and as she'd said to him, alive!

It was close to fully dark now, and though the night would give him cover it also meant that Jacob had to pick his away with care. He moved slowly, but steadily, covering ground at a good pace, and Jacob judged it to be around eight o'clock when he first saw the lights of Bannock ahead of him.

He moved in as close to town as he could, giving himself ample time to reach the first building. From there he checked the surrounding area for any sign of Will's men; they'd be around somewhere he was certain. They might have reasoned that Jacob could return to Bannock, and if they had he was going to have to walk easy.

On his journey back to Bannock, Jacob had noticed a sudden rise of wind. Now it was driving in steadily, sweeping down out of the high northern peaks, and almost as he took note of the wind he felt the first drops of rain. Swiftly now the drops increased. Within a couple of minutes Jacob was soaked to the skin as the dark skies opened and the rain, driven by the wind, lashed down on to the wide land.

Jacob watched the street empty as men took to the boardwalks and then to the bright warmth of the saloon and the gambling halls. He waited until Bannock's main street became empty, the only sound the drum of the rain on the roof-tops. And still he waited, watching, patient, because he knew that if he wasn't he could end up dead this night.

And eventually he saw them. Two men carrying rifles. They moved out of the shadows down the street, and from where he was Jacob could see that they appeared to be interested in one particular building. Moving along the opposite boardwalk, keeping in the shadows, Jacob finally drew level with the building; it faced him from the other side of the street and by the pale glow from lamps, even through the downpour, he saw the sign above the door: The Calico Restaurant. It seemed to Jacob that he'd guessed right. He'd found the right place, now all he had to do was to get inside.

One of the riflemen walked into a pool of lamplight and Jacob caught sight of a face he knew — the deputy called Jackson. Jacob stayed where he was, giving himself time to study the lie of the land; he needed to know the routine of the two deputies across the street before he made any attempt to get into the restaurant.

And suddenly Jackson turned and started across the street, his way bringing him towards the place where Jacob stood. For a moment Jacob thought he'd been spotted, but then he took note of Jackson's manner, the slow, casual pace, and realised that the man was simply crossing the street, most probably to check the area. As he watched the deputy approach Jacob's mind worked rapidly and he found himself formulating a rough plan of action. If it came off he might have found himself a way across the street and into the restaurant.

Jackson stepped up on to the boardwalk, facing away from Jacob; the deputy paused to take off his rain-sodden hat, shaking off the surplus water. In that moment Jacob stepped out of the deep shadows and laid the barrel of his Colt across the back of

Jackson's head. The deputy grunted and dropped to his knees. Jacob hit him again and Jackson pitched forward onto his face. Jacob dragged him across the boardwalk and into the nearest alley. Using Jackson's own belt and kerchief, Jacob bound and gagged the unconscious deputy, then propped him up behind a pile of empty barrels. Picking up Jackson's rifle Jacob started across the street.

Jackson's partner had moved out of sight down the side of the restaurant; as Jacob stepped into the alley he saw the man leaning against the wall of the restaurant, in the process of lighting a cigarette. Moving swiftly down the alley Jacob was up to the man before the deputy realised. He sensed Jacob's presence too late. Jacob drove the butt of his rifle deep into the deputy's stomach. The man grunted and slumped to his knees. Jacob slammed the butt of the rifle down across the back of the man's head, pitching him face down in the rain-soaked dust.

The rear of the restaurant was a jumble of litter, overturned barrels and boxes. Jacob picked his way to the back door, tried the handle. The door was locked. Putting his shoulder to it Jacob thrust hard a couple of times. He felt the flimsy door give, heard the inside latch break free. He eased the door open and stepped inside. He was in the kitchen. To his right the cooking range gave off a soft orange glow and somewhere coffee was brewing gently, the aroma tying Jacob's empty stomach in knots.

Jacob made his way across the kitchen, coming out into a narrow hall. He could see the restaurant's front window. Jacob turned away from there, moving down the hall. At the end was a door. Beneath the door he could see a band of light. He paused by the door. He'd know shortly whether he'd guessed right or not. If the girl wasn't in there he was going to have to move out of here fast.

Jacob knew there was no point in

hesitating. The sooner he made his move the better. Reaching down Jacob grasped the door handle and eased it free from the latch. He put his foot against the door and pushed it open.

The girl recognised him straightaway. She stepped forward and took his arm, leading him into the small room, closing the door behind him. Jacob leaned back against the wall, feeling weariness come on him again.

'You're hurt,' he heard her say. 'Come over here and sit down.'

'No time,' Jacob said. 'I've got to get you out of here.'

'You saw them outside? Jackson and Thatcher?'

Jacob nodded. 'You're as much a danger to them now as I am. They'll hesitate a while over harming a woman, but they'll come after you in the end. It's because of me you're in this trouble so it's up to me to get you out.'

'It's been coming a long time,' she said. 'Ever since Will was made marshal. My father was the Law in

Bannock before Will came, but he died. And I never did cotton to Will, even from the start. And when those robberies began I started to get the notion that Will knew a lot more about them than anybody realised. Maybe I was just watching him closer than most folk. But I couldn't take to him, and when he gathered that wild bunch round him I just got suspicious. Comes of having a lawman in the family. There always seemed to be some of his men out of town whenever a robbery took place, and they're never short of money. Trouble is I couldn't tell anybody what I thought. There was nobody to tell. Bannock's full of people too busy to bother, and anyway, the town's so grateful for the way Will and his boys keep it peaceful, I doubt if they'd believe me.'

'Sounds like Will has the town in his pocket,' Jacob said.

'He figures he's the big man. Anything he wants he can take!' Her voice was suddenly bitter.

'Sounds like something personal.'

She glanced at him, her eyes bright with anger. 'He tried to rape me! Came in here one night, half-drunk, saying he was going to do me a big favour. Now he was wearing the badge my father wore. He figured he ought to keep it in the family. He was lucky. My finger was trembling on the trigger of the shotgun I keep handy and I nearly gave him both barrels. He went out of here thinking I'd showed how tough I was. Truth is I was scared silly.'

She stopped speaking then, her eyes searching his face, as if she were looking for something missing out of her life.

'I'll get ready,' she said then.

As she turned away Jacob reached out and touched her arm. 'What do I call you?' he asked, and she smiled, the tension slipping away from her face.

'Hannah,' she said. 'Hannah Crane.'

She was back in a few minutes, dressed in faded Levis and wearing a thick coat. A pair of saddlebags and a blanket roll were slung over one arm.

'That's all,' she said.

'What about this place?' Jacob asked. He'd gone into the kitchen and helped himself to a mug of the brewed coffee, lacing it with plenty of sugar.

Hannah glanced up from filling an empty flour sack with supplies from the kitchen shelves. 'I only work here. When my father died I had to earn my own living. Cooking was one thing I did well. Too well for this place.'

She tied the sack and joined Jacob by the stove. 'Are you sure you can make it? Jacob, you look terrible.'

'Well, I feel terrible.' He drained his coffee. 'Right now there's no chance of doing anything about it. It's not going to be long before Will and his boys get round to us, so we'd better move while we can.'

They left the restaurant by the back door, making their way along the backlots toward the livery. The minutes seemed to fly by, and the longer it took the more worried Jacob became. Sooner or later the two men he'd downed were going to be discovered, and once that happened Bannock would become a hard place to get out of.

There was another of Will's deputies outside the livery. Jacob didn't spend too much time debating what to do. He left Hannah in the shadows and walked openly across the rain-drenched street towards the livery. The deputy watched him, but did nothing until Jacob reached the livery door.

'Hey, mister!' the deputy called and walked towards Jacob.

Jacob turned towards the man slowly, making no sudden move, letting the deputy get to within a few feet. And then the rifle, which Jacob had held out of sight against his body, swung up and round, the barrel catching the deputy under the chin. The man grunted hoarsely, the impact of the blow sending him crashing back against the livery wall before he crashed down on to the muddy ground.

Hannah joined Jacob and they

slipped into the silent livery. While Hannah went to saddle her horse, Jacob saw to his own animal; it took some doing throwing his heavy saddle into place; pain tore through his arm and shoulder, and Jacob knew that he was going to have to have something done soon. He finished off the job in a strained silence, his face glistening with sweat.

Hannah rejoined him, leading her horse, a long-legged black. He handed her the rifle he'd taken from Jackson; his own rifle was in its scabbard on his saddle. They mounted up and rode out of the livery into the rain-swept night.

'Hannah,' Jacob said suddenly, 'what do you know about this witness Will has? The one supposed to have seen me on one of the robberies?'

'Charlie Meeker,' Hannah said. 'He's the company agent who runs the stage swing-station up on High Ridge. It's about three hours ride north.'

'I'd like to have a few words with Charlie Meeker,' Jacob said. 'Maybe give him a chance to change his mind, and help him if he has difficulty.'

It took them slightly longer than three hours to reach High Ridge. The rainstorm increased as they left Bannock behind them, and as their way took them steadily upwards towards the distant peaks, they found themselves riding straight into the storm. The rain and wind tore at them, soaking their clothing, numbing them with cold.

Just on midnight they were forced to call a halt and to take shelter in a rocky outcrop. Riding deep into the fall of boulders and rocks they dismounted and huddled together for warmth. Despite the cold Jacob decided against lighting a fire; they could have used the warmth, both for themselves and to heat some coffee, but Jacob knew that by now Will would be trailing them, and he didn't want to risk giving Will any indication as to their whereabouts.

Jacob could imagine Will's state of mind right now. With Jacob free and still alive, Will would be facing the prospect of his setup in Bannock coming out into the open. And that would be enough to spur him on to any lengths to try and stop Jacob before he managed to reach anyone ready to listen to his story. The fact that Hannah was with Jacob would also add to Will's anger; two people telling the same story had more weight than one, and the fact that Hannah was the daughter of Bannock's late marshal would help too.

Jacob realised that he and Hannah were probably in more danger right now than they had been before leaving Bannock. Will and his bunch would be ready to shoot on sight to silence the two people who could expose their crimes.

The storm held its fury as the night dragged by. The hours drifted by with agonising slowness. Jacob, his body weak, shivering with cold, fell into a restless sleep. Hannah eased him to the ground and held him in her arms, feeling the ragged shudders that racked his body. She took her blanket roll and covered him, hoping that it might provide some warmth.

It was only with the grey light of dawn that the storm began to recede. The wind eased off and the rain faded away to a light drizzle that looked like mist on the higher slopes above them.

Hannah woke out of a light sleep with a sudden start, realising where she was. She sat up, stretching her aching body. She was hungry and cold, her clothes damp and uncomfortable, but they were things she could put up with. Turning, she bent over Jacob and was relieved to see him awake; he was pale, but his eyes were clear and sane, and she realised that he was out of the fever that had held him during the night.

'Any sign of them?' he asked. He sat up slowly. He was weak and a little sick, and he wasn't fooling himself — if he didn't get his shoulder seen to soon he was going to suffer a hell of a sight more than he had last night.

They took their horses out onto the trail again and Hannah pointed the way. High Ridge swing-station lay just under an hour ahead of them.

Jacob wondered how he would go about getting Meeker to admit he'd lied. Even if he did, what use would it be to him? Meeker was safe in his station up here. The only way to prove his claim against Meeker, and also Will, was to get his evidence to some regular lawman. That meant taking Meeker to the nearest town and getting him to tell the truth in front of a marshal or sheriff.

High Ridge lived up to its name. The swing-station was built on a narrow strip of land at the crest of a long rise. Here, when a stage had negotiated the tortuous climb, the team would be changed for a fresh set of horses for the next leg of the journey. There was little to the place; the station-house, a stable, corral, and a couple of small outhouses.

They drew rain on the crest of the rise and looked down at the station. Smoke rose from the house. The corral was empty. A shutter on the house gently swung to and fro making a faint sound in the mountain fastness.

'Looks damn quiet,' Jacob said. He scanned the station yard and the stable, but saw nothing. 'Either Meeker's a late riser or . . . '

'Or there's trouble down there?' Hannah said.

Jacob smiled at her. 'Only one way to find out.' He slid his rifle out and checked the action, holding the rifle against his hip as he urged his horse on down the slope.

They rode across the muddy yard, drawing rein outside the house. Jacob took time to glance around before he swung down out of the saddle. Maybe he was being a damn fool, riding in like this, but he had to carry through this thing concerning Meeker; riding away from it wouldn't solve a thing; and there was no guarantee that he might not meet worse trouble if he did ride away.

The door of the house was off the latch. Jacob eased it open with his foot and stepped inside. He held his rifle up and ready.

Hannah had described Charlie Meeker to him, and the man on the floor of the station-house fitted that description perfectly. Only the bald head differed — where there should have been the top of Meeker's head there was now a bloody mess of shattered bone and flesh and brains. Somebody had very neatly blown the top of Meeker's head off. Jacob looked at the man and felt sickness rise up in him; Will had anticipated this move; he must have reasoned that Jacob would learn the identity of the man supposed to have identified him, and that Jacob would try and find Meeker. It seemed that Will was well ahead of the game.

Jacob spun away from Meeker and headed for the door, knowing that there could be very real danger if he and

Hannah stayed on here too long. Meeker no longer meant anything to Jacob, so there was no use in staying around waiting for Will to arrive.

Jacob heard the crack of the gun, the thud of the bullet slamming into the doorframe inches from his face. He dropped to a crouch, grabbing the reins of his horse.

'Kick 'em up,' he said to Hannah as he dragged himself into the saddle. 'And keep your head down!'

She obeyed him without question, drumming her heels into her horse's sides, sending it skittering across the yard, with Jacob in close pursuit. Jacob heard the hidden gun fire again and realised it was coming from off to his right. He took a quick glance in that direction and saw the faintest wisp of powdersmoke. The gunman was standing in the shadow thrown by the high stable. In the instant that Jacob looked, the gunman fired again, the bullet clipping the horn of Jacob's saddle. He was getting closer, Jacob realised.

He hauled in on his reins, swinging his horse around to face the gunman. Driving the horse forward Jacob upped his rifle and started shooting. The rapid-action of the rifle sent a hail of bullets into the shadowed place where the gunman was hiding.

Moments later Jacob saw the man run out into the open. He recognised the deputy named Jackson; there must have been a faster route to the swing-station to enable Jackson to get here so quickly; Jacob cursed the ill-luck that had forced him to sleep through the night; if he hadn't caught that bullet in his shoulder he would have ridden without pause to the station.

Out of the corner of his eye Jacob saw movement over by the corral. He threw a quick glance in that direction and saw a second figure running across the yard; this man wore a badge and he was carrying a Colt Revolving Rifle.

Jacob reined in hard and kicked his feet free from the stirrups as he saw this second man raise the rifle and take aim. Forgetting the pain in his shoulder Jacob threw himself out of the saddle. As he struck the ground, rolling away from his horse he heard the Colt rifle crack. Then it fired again, the bullet kicking up mud into his face. Jacob twisted round frantically, pushing his rifle forward, his finger easing back on the trigger. He blinked mud out of his eyes and saw the distant figure of the gunman through a watery curtain. Jacob eased right back on the trigger, felt the rifle kick back, heard the crash of the shot. The gunman stopped dead in his tracks, his head snapping back in a scarlet spray as Jacob's bullet tore through his face. The rifle spun from his fingers as he took a half-step to the right before plunging face down in the mud.

Pushing to his feet Jacob turned, searching for Jackson. He saw a dark shape rounding the far side of the house and went after it. As he reached the corner a gun blasted, the bullet ripping splinters of wood out of the log wall just above Jacob's head.

Jacob worked the rifle's lever, feeding a shell into the breech. He pushed away from the side of the house, stepping into the open, the rifle up and ready. Jackson, was there, facing Jacob, his handgun cocked and ready. But Jacob fired first, his finger drawing back the rifle's trigger a split-second before Jackson could fire. The bullet caught Jackson just above the belt-buckle, spinning him round. Jackson lost his footing and went down on one knee, clutching a hand to his bleeding body. Yet even now he tried to lift his gun again, his face taut with mixed anger and strain. Jacob tilted the muzzle of the rifle and put a second bullet into the man, pitching him face down in the mud.

Jacob leaned against the side of the house. He was feeling weak again. His head ached badly and the pain in his shoulder was increasing fiercely. He stared at Jackson's blood-spattered body and a great bitterness came over him; he'd come here hoping to clear things up and instead the matter had got out of hand.

He glanced up as Hannah reached him. She touched his arm, her eyes searching his haggard face.

'Meeker. They've killed him,' she said.

'He planned to have me put down for that,' he said. 'Jackson and the other one were waiting to gun me down 'in the act'. Will would have cleared things up nice and tidy. Me out of his hair. Meeker dead in case he decided to open his mouth.'

Hannah asked: 'What about me?'

Jacob didn't answer. There was no need to. They both knew the answer. Hannah had chosen her side, had shown herself against Will, so she was marked as he was.

'Let's get the hell out of here,' he said.

They mounted up and rode out, angling south now. Hannah wasn't sure where they were going.

They reached a stand of trees above the station. Jacob drew rein, holding onto his saddlehorn to keep himself upright. Hannah edged her horse closer to him, worry showing on her face.

'I want you away from Will,' Jacob said, 'but I ain't going to get far like this, Hannah.'

She dismounted quickly, freeing his coiled rope from his saddle. Working calmly she tied Jacob to his saddle. As she remounted she noticed that Jacob seemed to have lost consciousness. He'd rolled forward against the ropes that Hannah had tied round him. Hannah took hold of the reins of his horse and rode up the slope beyond the trees.

In her mind was only one thought: to get herself and Jacob away from here, somewhere, anywhere away from Will and his gang. And to Hannah that meant only one place in the near territory.

She put the horses up the wet slopes,

heading for a distant place where the trees and grass gave way to a sprawling rock-field where their passing would leave no tracks. And beyond there, in amongst the criss-cross canyons and ravines she knew a place where they could hole up; Will and his gang would never find them there Hannah knew. It was a deep hidden place known only to her father and herself. Years back, when he'd first come to this country her father had come upon this hidden canyon while searching for a wanted man. There was grass and water, a natural refuge from the elements and man. Close by a stand of trees was a small cabin, built maybe thirty years back by some long-dead loner. Here, Hannah decided, she and Jacob could hide.

It was well into the afternoon when they reached the narrow fissure of rock that marked the entrance to Hannah's canyon; to anyone not having knowledge of its existence there would be little chance of them spotting it, for by the very nature of the rock face, the creases and breaks, the fissure blended in as to be practically invisible.

Far, far below them Will and his bunch rode back and forth across the wide rock-field. Hannah had seen them hours back and she'd been able to hide herself and Jacob before they'd been spotted. Now, up here, there was little chance of anyone seeing them, and once they were in the canyon danger was completely past for the present.

She took the horses into the canyon. After the first few hundred yards it widened out. At the far end, some two miles away, the canyon spread to its widest. Here it spanned a good mile, ringed on all sides by high cliff walls.

Hannah was deeply worried about Jacob now. He'd come round once or twice, his face creased with pain, glistening with sweat, and she knew he was in fever again. She'd noticed that blood was soaking through the thick coat he wore. The bullet needed to come out of him quickly. Infection might have set in already. As she led the horses into the canyon Jacob lay forward across his saddle, silent and motionless; his only words during the whole ride had been some mumbled words about a town called Hope and someone called Brigham.

She saw the cabin ahead of her through the drizzle. Reaching it she got down and pushed open the door, then went back and took down the blanket-rolls from both horses. Taking them inside the cabin she laid them on the low cot that stood against one wall. Outside again she untied the rope and dragged Jacob down off his horse. His weight was almost too much for her, but she struggled against it and dragged his limp form across the ground and into the cabin, rolling him face down on to the cot. Leaving him she went outside again and brought in their gear and supplies off the horses. She shut the door, crossed to the fireplace and set to making a fire.

While water boiled on the fire

Hannah cut away Jacob's shirt after she'd pulled his coat off. She was barely able to suppress her shock as she exposed the wound; it was a swollen and discoloured mass of flesh, oozing festered matter. She fought back the panic that began to rise, knowing that she needed steady nerves and a steadier hand; she'd never taken a bullet out of anyone, but she'd seen it done a number of times.

In Jacob's saddlebags she'd found a slim, keen-bladed knife. She heated the blade in the flames to clean it, noticing that her hands were surprisingly steady. Behind her she heard Jacob groan and she prayed that she wasn't too late.

Will Retford had won this round. Hannah hoped that Jacob's struggle hadn't been in vain. He deserved another chance to put things to rights. If things turned out right here, then maybe he'd get it.

Hannah picked up the boiled water and went back to the cot. She sat down on the edge, the knife held in her hand.

She noticed the stillness that had come over Jacob and alarm grew in her. Bending over him she finally detected his shallow breathing. He was worse than she had realised. Hannah sleeved sweat from her face. She took a firm grip on the knife in her hand and leaned over Jacob, hoping and praying that she was still going to be in time.

18

Seth Tyler glanced up as a shadow fell across his desk. He narrowed his eyes against the bright sunlight gleaming through the open door of the jail, and saw the tall, lean figure stepping into the office.

He recognised the dark-suited, taut-featured man at first glance, and knew that U.S. Marshal Alvin LeRoy could only mean trouble.

'Mind if I step inside?' LeRoy asked.

Seth leaned back in his seat. He watched LeRoy cross the jail and sit down on a chair facing the desk.

'Heard from your brother lately?' LeRoy asked.

'Jacob?' Seth shook his head. 'Not for a few weeks. You lost track of him, Marshal?'

'I have information as to his whereabouts. Somewhere in Wyoming. Up in the Tetons.'

'Why are you telling me, LeRoy?'

LeRoy sat forward. 'He may be heading this way. No telling he won't get by me and trail in here. If he does it's up to you to keep him 'til I get back.'

'You serious, LeRoy?' Seth asked.

'That badge on your shirt don't say Ladies Sewing Circle.' LeRoy stood up, anger paling his face. 'You got a special set of laws for your own?'

'LeRoy, you may figure yourself a big man behind that fancy title, but you been pushing this thing for a long time. Maybe it's right you should stop and think before you go any further.'

'You figure your brother's innocent. I expect that. But I was there when it happened, and Virgil Boone was dead. And your brother ran. Not the way of a man who hasn't done anything.'

'Hell, LeRoy, is that all it takes for you to want to hang a man? What about the dead girl? You think Jacob killed her too?'

'That part I'm not clear on. But I

know there was something between Boone and your brother, something that led to Boone dying.'

'What about Will Retford? You still saying he doesn't exist?'

'You tell me. I didn't see him. You didn't.' LeRoy reached into his coat and took out a folded paper. He opened it and laid it on Seth's desk. 'I work on facts, Tyler. Facts like this poster.'

Seth found himself reading a 'Wanted' poster. The man's description and the sketch described Jacob. The poster said that Jacob was wanted for robbery and murder, and it had been issued by the marshal of a town in Wyoming, a town called Bannock.

'Seems your brother's branching out,' LeRoy said.

'I don't believe a word of it,' Seth said. He thrust up out of his seat. 'LeRoy, if I hear you're railroading Jacob, the whole damn U.S. marshal's office won't be big enough to stop me finding you!'

'I'm riding up to Bannock,' LeRoy

said. 'I'll decide what the truth is. If your brother's not guilty I'll not let him carry the blame. But if he is, Tyler, then he's a dead man already!'

LeRoy turned and left the jail. Seth stood in the doorway and watched the man cross the street and push his way through the crowds of men outside one of Hope's saloons. For a time he stood in the doorway, his mind busy with thoughts of Jacob. It seemed that there was always some problem arising, hardly giving a man time to breathe, and today's was Marshal Alvin LeRoy bringing grim news concerning Jacob.

Seth turned back into the office. He strapped on his gun, picked up his hat and rifle and strode out onto the street. He wanted to find Jules, his deputy, and to see his girl, Beth. He had some riding to do and he wanted to get started. It was a long ride up to Wyoming, and when he got there he still had to find Jacob.

★ ★ ★

(At the end of the first week) Jacob was able to take a walk outside the cabin unaided. It felt good to be out in the open air again) to feel the warm sun on his face. He walked as far as the small stream that ran nearby and knelt down, scooping up handfuls of the cool, fresh water to rinse his face. He was able to stand and look up at the blue sky beyond the trees and the high canyon wall.

He heard sound behind him and turned. It was Hannah. She had his soap and razor in her hands, and a pan of hot water. 'There's a handy rock behind you,' she said. 'Sit down.'

Jacob sat, watching her as she set the things out on the ground. He put a hand to his face and felt the thick beard that had grown.

'I must look like hell on a rough Sunday,' he said.

'Not to me,' was her reply, looking him straight in the eye. 'Sit still!'

Jacob sat motionless while she soaped and shaved him. Afterwards she washed

283

off the remaining lather and dried his face with a towel she'd brought.

'Feels better,' he said approvingly.

Hannah laughed softly, and then suddenly she stepped up to him and kissed him, her soft lips closing fully on his own. Jacob reached out and held her, not wanting to release her, his senses reacting to her womanly shape.

'Hey!' Hannah eased herself out of his grip, her cheeks flushing hotly. 'You are still weak.'

'You sure?' Jacob asked; but he knew the answer. He was still weak. Even now, after only a short time outside, he was beginning to feel tired. The bullet he'd carried, and the infection it had left him with, had robbed him of a great amount of blood and a lot of strength, and it was all taking a deal of regaining.

They returned to the cabin and Hannah poured out some coffee. They sat in silence for a time. Then Hannah said: 'We need more food, Jacob. You could do with some meat.'

'We won't get it round here.'

'But I could get it from Holland,' Hannah said.

'Where's that?'

'Town about a half-day's ride south. Not a big place, but it has a couple of stores. I could pick up pretty well everything we need. Food, extra clothing.'

'Let you go on your own?' Jacob shook his head. 'I won't let you, Hannah!'

She put a hand on his. 'Be practical, Jacob. We need the stuff. You can't go. Your poster's plastered all over the county by now. And you're in no fit state to ride yet. You need a few more days, and you also need some good food inside you.'

Jacob knew she was right. He had to give her that. Hannah had been right all the way along the line since they'd come here. She'd chosen a good place for them to hide. She'd taken out the bullet in his shoulder, cleaning up the poisoned wound, sitting with him day and night while his body had burned with fever. He had a lot to thank her for, and the way things were he was going to have to thank her again.

'When would you go?' he asked.

'First light,' she said. 'I can be back by evening!'

Next morning she was up before it was light. She lighted the fire and made them breakfast and coffee. Afterwards she got herself ready for the ride to Holland, went outside and saddled her horse.

Jacob handed her a fold of bank-notes. 'Get whatever we need,' he said. 'And go careful. Will and his boys may still be around.'

'Oh, I'm very careful,' she said.

Jacob smiled at her. He reached out and took her in his arms, kissing her long and hard. It was actually their first physical contact since coming to the canyon; there had been little time before; most of the time Jacob had been sleeping or in the grip of fever; but here, now, there was no concealing the feelings he had for Hannah, and to his delight she responded eagerly.

'No more, Jacob,' she said. 'Not now. Else I never will get to Holland!'

He watched her go until she was out of sight, then went back inside the cabin. He stared around the small room, seeing nothing that he might pass the time with. Restlessly Jacob paced the cabin. It was going to be a long, long day, he realised, and he was going to miss that girl!

*　*　*

Hannah was back well before he'd expected her; as she flung herself down out of the saddle he noticed that her horse was bathed in sweat and was breathing hard.

'We've got to move,' she said. 'Jacob, I'm certain I've been followed back from Holland.'

'Will's boys?'

She shook her head. 'Worse. Benteen and Hinds. They're bounty-hunters, Jacob, the worst kind. Animals on two legs. My father had more than one run-in with them while he wore the badge in Bannock.'

'What happened?'

'I was just leaving Holland and they rode right by me. I knew they'd recognised me. As soon as I was out of town I rode hard, but I spotted a pair of riders following my trail when I started up into the hills.'

Jacob strapped on his gun and began to gather up their gear.

'You think they could find this place?'

Hannah nodded. 'If anybody could it's that pair.'

Mounting up they headed down the canyon, making for the narrow entrance that would take them out onto the side of the mountain. It would be dark in a couple of hours Jacob realised. Darkness might give them some cover, give them a chance to slip away; it depended on how good Benteen and Hinds were. If they knew the country well escape from them might prove a sight more difficult than he might think. But whatever happened they would have to act on the moment, planning as they went.

They broke out of the canyon, riding slowly along the narrow ledge that bordered the hidden mouth of the canyon. Taking their horses on to level ground they reined in for a moment.

'Where do we go, Jacob?' Hannah asked. 'I've nowhere else to suggest.'

'We head south,' he told her. 'For Colorado. Before I do anything else I want you out of harm's way. I'm taking you to my brother Brigham's ranch outside Hope. You'll be safe there. Seth will be on hand too.'

'I've become a burden to you, Jacob,' Hannah said.

He leaned across and touched her face. 'You can quit that kind of talk right now. If it hadn't been for you I'd be dead, and that means a lot, Hannah.'

They turned their horses, setting themselves along the trail. Jacob led, Hannah following a few yards behind. Easing down the slopes they made for the treeline that ran below them.

The two riders broke out of the trees while they were still a fair distance off. Jacob pulled his horse round, reaching for his sheathed rifle.

'It's them,' Hannah yelled. 'Benteen and Hinds!'

'Head for that ridge,' Jacob said, pointing to the place that lay off to their right.

Hannah spurred her horse forward. In that instant a rifle cracked harshly, the bullet kicking up dirt ahead of her.

'Keep going,' Jacob yelled. He turned in his saddle, bringing up his rifle. He squeezed the trigger, sending a bullet close to one of the bounty-hunters. The lead man hauled in on his reins, his startled horse rearing wildly, spilling him from the saddle. His partner, coming close on his heels, only just avoided trampling him.

Jacob, by this time, had turned his horse and was riding after Hannah, and they were up and over the ridge without another shot being fired. Beyond the ridge they hit a stretch of rocky country, a place where they would be able to reach the trees without breaking out of cover. It was only a brief spell of comparative safety before Benteen and Hinds rode after them. Jacob hoped they could build up a good lead before darkness fell. The more distance he put between Hannah and himself, and the bounty-hunters, the better he would feel.

★ ★ ★

They rode throughout the night, taking more chances than Jacob would have done at any other time. But he wanted to lose Benteen and Hinds if he possibly could, though he began to have doubts that he would.

Jacob found he was tiring very quickly; he realised that Hannah had been right — he still needed rest — but he knew that there was no chance of that now. They had to keep moving, try to reach Hope.

As dawn broke they were riding down through the foothills. Light flooded the dark land, pushing back the shadows, and when Jacob drew rein, looking back up into the hills they'd just descended, he could see the distant figures of the two bounty-hunters.

Hannah had seen them too. 'They've been known to dog a man until he just ups and quits. And then they'll ride in and finish him off!'

'Not this one,' Jacob said.

They rode on, into a day that promised to be a hot one. They were both hungry, but they contented themselves with water from their canteens and chunks of cheese, which they ate as they rode.

As their horses crested a long slope, taking them to the fringe of a dense thicket, there was a sudden flurry of movement off to one side. A horse and rider burst into view, right in their path.

And Jacob found himself staring into the muzzle of a sawn-off shotgun held in the hands of U.S. marshal Alvin LeRoy.

'Don't make me use it, Tyler,' LeRoy snapped. 'At this range I couldn't help but hit the lady as well!'

Jacob slumped forward in his saddle, his weariness suddenly catching up on him; if he'd been alone he might have chanced something, but he knew that with Hannah by his side there was no chance at all.

'Hands away from your sides,' LeRoy said. 'Both of you! Until I know just how deep you're in this, ma'am I'm taking no chances.'

He dismounted, still holding the shotgun on them, moving quickly round their horses as he disarmed them both.

'Ma'am, put out your right hand.'

Hannah did as she was told and LeRoy snapped the jaws of a set of handcuffs on to her wrist, turning the key to lock it. Jacob was told to offer his left hand, and he too felt the cold metal encircle his wrist, heard the click of it locking.

'You led me a long chase, Tyler,'

LeRoy said as he mounted up. 'But it's over now, boy, and I'll see you behind bars this time.'

'Do I get a chance to tell my side of it?' Jacob asked.

'In court, boy, in court,' LeRoy said. 'My job is to catch felons. It's up to somebody else to decide your guilt!'

'Or innocence!' Hannah said hotly.

LeRoy glanced at her, his hard face made harder by the cold smile. A smile that didn't reach his bitter eyes. 'As you say, little lady. Only this time I have more than a passing interest in the case. Being more-or-less a witness.'

'Hell, no!' Jacob exploded. 'Damn you, LeRoy, you're a liar!'

'Easy, boy, less I happen to nudge the trigger on this scattergun!'

'That would be murder, Marshal,' Hannah said, her gaze fixed solidly on LeRoy's face.

'Would it, ma'am?' he asked coldly, his tone and implication sending a shiver down her spine.

They moved out at his bidding,

retracting their steps. Jacob had a feeling that LeRoy was taking them back to Bannock. Maybe, just maybe, he might be able to salvage something from this mess yet. LeRoy obviously didn't know about Will Retford's pose as the marshal of Bannock. Jacob decided not to say anything about it. A sudden confrontation might be just the thing to upset Will's masquerade.

But fate had decided otherwise and Jacob's hopes for a return to Bannock were rudely shattered by the appearance of Benteen and Hinds. The two bounty-hunters suddenly rode into view, drawing rein across the path of LeRoy and his prisoners.

'Well now, Marshal,' the one called Hinds said, 'it 'pears Dave an' me got to say thanks to you.'

'For what?' LeRoy asked.

Benteen, a tall, thickset man with black, tangled hair, grinned, showing large, yellow teeth. 'Why Marshal, for catching our two runaways fo' us. We been after 'em a time. And you gone an' caught 'em all nice an' easy!'

'Bounty-hunters!' LeRoy spat the words out as realisation came to him. He sat up in his saddle, his body rigid. 'I have one thing to say to you two. Step out of my way. I'm a U.S. marshal, and these two are my prisoners. Make any kind of move and you buy a lot of trouble!'

Benteen laughed softly. 'You got it all wrong, Marshal! There's a fat reward out fo' this here Tyler feller, an' me an' Ike have staked our claim. Now I don't give a hatful of shit for your badge. Won't mean a thing when you-all is dead. An' this pair ain't goin' to do no talkin' on it, 'cause that 'Wanted' flyer says 'Alive or Dead'!'

With his last words spoken Benteen leaned to one side, and LeRoy saw that the other man, Hinds, had a gun in his hand, previously hidden by Benteen's bulk. The gun was already levelled and cocked, and LeRoy was far too late to aim his shotgun before Hinds fired. The gun, a heavy Dragoon Colt, roared, spitting flame and smoke, and LeRoy felt a stunning impact as the bullet hit him. He was pushed back out of his saddle. He hit the ground hard, the back of his head striking the ground and he knew no more as everything went black around him.

As Hinds fired and the Dragoon exploded, Jacob knew that he and Hannah had little time left; once they'd done with LeRoy, the bounty-hunters would turn on him and Hannah. If he was going to do something it had to be now and it had to be fast, no matter how slim a chance it might offer.

With that in mind Jacob kicked his feet free from the stirrups, thrusting his body from the saddle.

'Hannah!' he yelled. 'Down!'

She responded to his call, following him to the ground. Momentarily shielded by their horses they ran forward, Jacob practically dragging Hannah by the short length of chain that joined their wrists. He knew where they were headed, hoping that they might reach it before Benteen and Hinds got a clear shot at them.

A few yards away the ground fell away in a long, steep slope to the bottom of some long-dead river-bed. If they could get over the edge and down the slope they might stand some kind of chance.

Even in the frantic rush to the edge of the drop, Jacob's eye was caught by the sight of LeRoy's body hitting the ground only feet away. As LeRoy struck the earth, his arms were flung wide by the impact, and the shotgun, clutched in one hand, flew free from his nerveless fingers, skidding in the dust almost at Jacob's feet. And in a reflex action Jacob reached out and closed his hand around the weapon.

Behind them came a sudden yell of anger. Following close on the yell came the boom of the big Dragoon. Jacob heard the bullet slam into hard ground close by. But then they were on the edge of the drop. Jacob didn't hesitate. He thrust Hannah over the edge, going over after her.

The slope was steep and soft underfoot. Held together by the manacles they hurtled down the slope in a billowing cloud of thick dust and rattling shale. Their bodies spun and twisted over and over, bruised and scraped by the headlong fall.

Yet the very dust that threatened to choke them also hid them from the sight of Benteen and Hinds.

They hit bottom hard, Jacob momentarily losing his grip on the shotgun. He grabbed it up again as he shoved to his feet, grasping Hannah's wrist and pulling her with him. They ran. Hard and fast, heading along the river-bed. Jacob had no particular destination. All he wanted to do was to get out of range of the guns of Benteen and Hinds.

Shots rang out behind them, bullets whipping through the air close by them; but the swirling dust caused by their descent still fogged the river-bed, making them hard targets.

Jacob knew it wouldn't be long

before Benteen and Hinds came down after them, and all he had was a shotgun; he paused long enough to check the loads and found that both barrels were primed.

As they ran, rounding a sharp curve in the river bed, he saw a narrow fissure in the bank; in the time when the river had flowed this fissure would have fed it with water coming down out of the distant hills. Jacob pointed it out to Hannah and they headed into the fissure, finding themselves in a narrow gully. As they moved into it they found that it was extremely rough underfoot, and the gully itself was thickly choked with tangled brush. It caught in their clothing, the thorny branches scratching their faces. But they pushed on, ignoring the pain and the discomfort, because they knew that they had little choice; no matter how bad their position was here it could never be as bad as the other option — in the forms of Benteen and Hinds.

They forced their way along the gully

for more than a mile, and suddenly found it levelling out until it merged with the surrounding land. They found themselves on open, flat ground, abruptly and badly exposed.

There was no sign of Benteen and Hinds, but Jacob knew that the bounty-hunters would be around somewhere. They wouldn't give up easily. Not with money riding on Jacob's capture — dead or alive!

'Rest a minute,' he said, pulling Hannah down beside him.

Hannah slumped down onto the ground. She was bathed in sweat, her breathing harsh and ragged. Jacob noticed that her manacled wrist was chafed raw and bloody by the rough iron bracelet.

About to speak he suddenly noticed a faint swirl of dust from a high ridge behind them. A moment later a horse and rider crested the ridge. Although the man was a fair distance away Jacob recognised him — it was Benteen.

'Damn!'

Hannah turned her head to see what he was looking at and saw Benteen. The bounty-hunter saw them too. Sunlight flashed on his rifle as he lifted it to his shoulder.

Jacob threw himself at Hannah, the force of his drive knocking her flat. And as he went down beside her he heard the vicious crack of the distant rifle. The bullet tugged his shirt as it passed, raising a ball of dust as it struck the ground inches away.

Grabbing Hannah's wrist Jacob dragged her along the ground, praying for some kind of cover. There seemed to be little here. The ground was flat and open.

Benteen's rifle fired again. This second bullet went wide. Benteen didn't seem to be too good a shot, but given time he would eventually hit one of them. Jacob hoped they could make some cover before that time came.

'Jacob!' Hannah's voice reached him and he turned his head. She was pointing off to the right.

He glanced that way and saw another

gully, similar to the one they'd used recently. It had been hidden from them by a shallow dip in the ground, but now they were very close to it. Jacob turned his prone body that way. He threw a quick look towards Benteen and saw that the man was much closer now.

'Up on your feet!' he said to Hannah. 'And run!'

They reached the gully with Benteen thundering across the flat towards them. Had he been a better shot they would never have reached it. As it was his bullets sang through the air all around them, but not one touched them.

The edge of the gully appeared at their feet and they plunged over without hesitation. Sliding and slipping on the steep shale they crashed into the brush-choked gully, pushing their way deep into the tangled growth.

Up on the gully rim Benteen emptied his rifle into the brush, cursing wildly. His bullets tore through the under-growth, the only one to do any kind of damage clipping Jacob's left arm in passing. It drew blood but little else.

As they had with the first gully, Jacob and Hannah just followed its course. This one twisted and bent its laborious way seemingly for mile after mile. They just carried on fighting their way through the undergrowth, oblivious to the time, the stifling heat and the choking, acid dust that swirled up from under their feet. They were soaked in sweat, their bodies cut and slashed by the cruel, thorny brush, yet they kept moving, knowing that if they stopped now they wouldn't have the strength to move on again.

It was Hannah who noticed the sky darkening above them, and the sudden lower temperature. The day was nearly over. The night was coming on, and they were still alive. Hungry, thirsty, tired and battered, but they were still alive!

She pulled Jacob to a stop, realising that he was practically asleep on his feet. He showed little resistance as she drew him into a shallow cave formed in the rocky section of the gully bank.

'Jacob,' she said. 'We can rest now. It's getting dark. We should be safe here.'

He glanced at her and she saw the fatigue in his face, and marvelled at the way he'd kept going all this time. He was still weak from his wound, yet he'd kept both of them moving, and Hannah knew that if it hadn't been for his stubborn determination they wouldn't have got this far.

With full darkness came the chilling cold of this high country. Hannah thought of the coats and blankets they'd carried on their horses, and the thought made her shiver. Jacob drew her close, holding her body against his for warmth.

'I might keep this chain on for good,' he told her. 'That way I won't lose you.'

Hannah laughed softly, her breath warm on his face. 'I like the idea, but wouldn't it get in the way on certain occasions?'

He was silent for a moment. Then his sleepy voice reached her. 'Easy way to find out,' he said.

* * *

In the grey light of early dawn they lay together, listening to the sound of slow-moving horses. There were two animals and they were being ridden back and forth along the banks of the gully.

Jacob knew who the riders were. Benteen and Hinds were still after that bounty-money. If they were nothing else they were consistent.

After a time the hoofbeats drifted away. But shortly one horse returned. It was reined in on the bank not far from where they were. Saddle-leather creaked as someone dismounted. Boots scraped the rock and a shower of small stones trickled down into the gully, hissing through the tangled brush. More scraping sounds followed, and further small avalanches of dust.

Hannah looked at Jacob, her eyes wide with alarm. He nodded to her, in silent answer to her unasked question; one of the bounty-hunters was coming down into the gully for a look round.

Jacob gripped the shotgun, making sure the hammers were down. He didn't want to fire the weapon if he could avoid it. There was no telling how close the other man might be.

Through the brush he spotted the dark figure of the bounty-hunter as he came down off the sloping bank. The man paused, looking round as if undecided which way to go. Then he began to push his way through the thick tangle, in a direction that would bring him right past the place where Jacob and Hannah were hiding.

Jacob readied himself. He could feel Hannah close behind him, her body held taut with the tension of the moment; she was completely opposite to the way she'd been the night before, in fact only short hours ago, when her lithe body had relaxed beneath him,

307

her warmth and need for him revealing itself in the strong passion that had quickened and heightened her responses.

The brush crackled and rustled as the bounty-hunter stepped closer. Jacob leaned out from the shallow cave and caught a quick glimpse of the man's dark-stubbled face. It was the one called Benteen. He had a Colt in one hand and the way he carried the gun it was plain that he knew how to use it.

Benteen was alongside the cave almost before Jacob realised it, but he reacted swiftly. As Benteen stepped by, thrusting aside the brush, Jacob moved out behind him and laid the shotgun barrel across the back of Benteen's head. The bounty-hunter pitched forward, slamming up against the gully side. The Colt dropped from his fingers, but Benteen didn't go down and Jacob realised that he hadn't hit the man hard enough; but he was still not fully recovered from the effects of the bullet wound; normally he could have dropped Benteen with one blow.

As Jacob stepped forward, Hannah following him, trying to match his pace, Benteen shoved away from the side, turning to face Jacob. The bounty-hunter saw nothing, except for the twin barrels of the shotgun, a split-second before it hit him, dropping him like a stone, blood streaming from his mouth.

Knowing there was little time to spare. Jacob knelt beside the unconscious bounty-hunter, unstrapping the gunbelt. He hung it around his own waist, dropping Benteen's Colt into the holster.

'You think you can handle this?' he asked, passing her the shotgun.

Hannah glanced at the weapon. 'If I need to!'

Without a backward glance at Benteen, Jacob led off along the gully. He retraced Benteen's steps until he reached the place where the bounty-hunter had come down the bank.

'We reach the top,' he said, 'keep low. The other one might be around.'

They climbed the bank slowly, their

progress hampered by the chain that joined them. More than once they lost their footing, sliding yards back down the slope before they could check their descent.

Reaching the rim finally they crouched below skyline, taking time to ease their heavy breathing. The day was lighting quickly now, the distant sky taking on a soft orange glow as the sun began to rise.

Jacob spotted Benteen's horse. It was tethered to a clump of brush some yards away from the edge of the gully. He scanned the surrounding terrain, his eyes searching for Benteen's partner, but Hinds was nowhere to be seen.

'Benteen's horse is close by,' he told Hannah. 'I can't see Hinds, but he might be around. Once we clear this rim we move fast. As soon as we reach the horse I'll go up first. Then you swing up behind me, and hang on, because we might have to light out kind of fast.'

He led her up onto level ground and

the moment they left the gully behind them they ran across to Benteen's horse. Jacob loosened the reins and swung up into the saddle. It was awkward getting Hannah up behind him because of the manacle-chain, but they finally managed it; Hannah put her right arm round his waist so that Jacob had reasonable use of his left hand; he used it to hold the reins, leaving his right hand free for the holstered Colt on his right hip.

He gigged the horse into movement. Hannah was silent for a while, and then she asked:

'Jacob, why are we going this way? This won't take us south!'

'No. But it'll take us back to Bannock!'

Hannah's body tensed. 'Back to Bannock? I thought you wanted to get away from Bannock?'

'Hell, I do, Hannah! But it won't work. I'm letting Will run me off. And that don't sit right with me. Damn it, Hannah, he's the guilty one, not me, and running away ain't going to get it cleared up! I've had enough of tracking Will over half the country. This time I'm going to finish it, one way or another!'

He felt her arms tighten around him. 'All right, Jacob. Whatever you say.'

Jacob turned his horse towards the hills and Bannock. He knew that once he reached Bannock it would be a make or break conflict. He'd had enough of this life, this running and hiding. He wanted the thing finished with, one way or another, even if he had to force a play. And this time there would be no place for Will Retford to run and hide!

* * *

Seth Tyler reined in and climbed down out of his saddle. He crossed over to the motionless figure lying by the side of the narrow trail. He'd recognised Alvin LeRoy even before he'd dismounted, and as he approached he wondered whether he'd find the man alive or dead.

The ride up from Hope had been long and tiring, and the last thing Seth had expected to see on this particular day was Alvin LeRoy, with a gunshot wound.

Seth knelt beside LeRoy, and saw straightaway that the marshal was still alive; LeRoy, though pale, was breathing strongly, but he was still unconscious. Seth checked the wound. The bullet had hit LeRoy in the chest, high on the left side, but instead of going straight in it had turned at a sharp angle, eventually going through LeRoy's left shoulder and coming out at the rear; LeRoy had lost a fair amount of blood, though when Seth examined the wound he found it clean.

It was getting on towards dark, and Seth knew that there was no point in trying to move LeRoy too far. He took a look around, seeking a place to make camp for the night. To one side of the trail the ground fell away into a dry river-bed. The far side of the trail gave way into wooded country and after a few minutes tramping around Seth found a reasonable place to make camp. He led his horse to the place and tethered it to a low branch. Then he went back and picked LeRoy up, carrying him to the campsite. He laid the marshal down and covered him with his own blankets. Setting-to, Seth gathered wood and built a fire. Once it was going he poured water into his coffee-pot and placed it over the flames.

He'd noticed a stream some way off. Taking his two big canteens he headed that way. Reaching the stream he hunkered down to fill the canteens. He heard a sound and glanced up, and found himself looking across the stream at three saddled horses; saddled but riderless. He crossed the stream, approaching the horses slowly. They stamped their feet restlessly, but stayed where they were. Seth gathered their reins and began to check the animals and the gear they carried. It didn't take him long to realise that the horses belonged to LeRoy and Jacob. The third rider was unknown to him, though Seth figured that the rider was a woman, by what he'd found in the saddlebags.

He returned to camp with the horses and the water. Tethering them beside his own he headed for the fire, and found Alvin LeRoy sitting up, his back against a tree.

'Had a feeling you'd followed me,' LeRoy said.

'I figured it was time I took a hand.'

LeRoy glanced at the coffee-pot bubbling on the fire. 'That looks about ready.'

Removing the pot Seth filled a couple of mugs. He handed one to LeRoy, then sat down.

'Who was it?'

'Couple of bounty-hunters. I'd just got the drop on your brother and the girl with him when this pair rode up. I read 'em the way it was, but it appears they didn't take me too serious. Next thing I knew one of them poked a gun at me and put a bullet in me.'

'I found your horse,' Seth said. 'And Jacob's two, so he must have got away.'

'Or he's dead. Those bounty-men looked the type who preferred dead captives.'

Seth drained his coffee. 'I'd say that he's still alive. Bounty-hunter has to have something to show to collect his money. Dead or alive. And that means horses to carry a prisoner — or a corpse.'

'So they could be anywhere,' LeRoy said. 'Tyler. Your brother and the girl. Before those bounty-hunters turned up I put manacles on them. It's not going to make it easy for them.'

'You sound like you're feeling sorry for Jacob.'

LeRoy held out his mug for a refill. 'I figure any man should get justice. No matter what he's done. But bounty-hunters shouldn't be wished on anyone. I still mean your brother to stand before a court. If he can prove I've been wrong then I'll be the first to shake his hand. If not, then I'll only have done my job.'

Before it got too dark Seth cleaned and bandaged LeRoy's shoulder. After he prepared a meal of beans and bacon for them both, and soon after that both of them turned in for the night.

Seth was up at first light. He cooked a quick breakfast, reboiled the coffee. By the time it was ready LeRoy was awake. The marshal took a slow walk round the camp; his shoulder was stiff and sore, he was feeling weak, but he was determined to carry on — next to losing a prisoner having one stolen from him was one of the ways to bring out LeRoy's inborn stubbornness, a trait that had earned him his reputation over the years.

As soon as they'd eaten and broken camp Seth and LeRoy returned to the spot where the bounty-hunters had first appeared. It didn't take LeRoy long to find the place where Jacob and Hannah had gone down into the river-bed. He made a note of the direction of their tracks, and then he and Seth rode along the rim of the bank, searching for the place where Jacob and Hannah had come out.

The tracks were easier to follow when they reached level ground. Now they found the tracks of two horses, overlaying the trail made by Jacob and Hannah. Moving on they spotted the place were the trail vanished into the gully, and again they followed the gully until they found the place where a horse had been tethered on the rim of the gully. One man had gone down the bank, but two people had come up and had mounted the horse.

'Seems they've got themselves a horse,' LeRoy said. 'Took off that way.'

He pointed. Seth followed the line of hoofprints. 'Tell me if I'm wrong, but isn't that the general direction of Bannock?'

LeRoy eased himself in the saddle. 'Yeah.'

They rode out, moving in the same direction as the tracks, LeRoy leading, Seth following on, the two spare horses following him on the end of a slack rope.

Seth had a feeling that there was going to be a showdown in Bannock, and he hoped that he'd get there in time. Jacob might be needing help.

19

Bannock's blacksmith had his place at one end of town, just before a corral-complex. It was early when Jacob and Hannah rode in, and when Jacob took the horse to the rear of the blacksmith's there was no sound or movement in the place.

They dismounted and Jacob tied the horse. The door to the workshop was unlocked. Inside he searched around until he found what he was looking for; a heavy chisel and a large hammer. He laid the chain on the anvil.

'Give me that,' Hannah said, taking the chisel from him. She positioned it on one of the links.

Jacob wrapped a piece of sacking around the head of the hammer to muffle the sound. It took more than five minutes to cut through the first half of the link, but Jacob forced himself to take it steady, despite his desire to get out of the place; he had a dislike of being hemmed in. His shoulder was playing up, too, aching badly through the effort he was putting into the hammering.

Finally it was done, the chain parted, though they wore the manacles around their wrists.

'I want you to take the horse and wait in that grove of trees just beyond town,' Jacob said.

'I'd rather stay,' Hannah protested, but she knew as she spoke that Jacob had made his decision.

'No! Hannah, things might get rough. I want you out of harm's way.'

She nodded agreement. 'All right, Jacob. Be careful.'

He watched her lead the horse towards the trees, and only when she was out of sight did he turn and start up towards town.

The jail was at the other end of Bannock. Jacob saw no one the whole walk up the street. Even before he reached the jail he began to suspect that it was deserted.

The jail was silent and empty. Jacob walked inside and stood in the centre of the office. Where was Will? And where were his deputies? It was unusual for an entire law force to be out of town at the same time. Maybe Will was still out scouring the hills looking for Jacob. Or maybe he'd taken fright and run. Jacob wondered if he'd come too late again. Had he let Will slip away once more?

Jacob stepped outside and stood on the edge of the boardwalk. He felt at a loss. He'd come to Bannock determined to settle with Will Retford once and for all, and now it seemed that Will had already left Bannock. But Jacob knew he could be wrong. Will might return to Bannock at any time. It was worth a wait.

Jacob went back inside the jail. The clock on the wall behind the desk read almost seven.

* * *

Hannah, well-concealed in the grove of trees, heard the single horse approaching down the trail that led into Bannock. From where she was she saw that the horse carried two riders, and she easily recognised the two bounty-hunters, Benteen and Hinds. She felt the cold chill that their presence always invoked. There was something evil, almost alien about them. As they rode by she found herself wondering about Jacob. She'd heard nothing since he had left her, and that was more than an hour ago. She was beginning to get worried. Where was Jacob? How was he?

She watched Benteen and Hinds riding slowly up the street. A few people were about now. The stores were beginning to open. Despite her promise to Jacob, Hannah felt she ought to go and warn him about the bounty-hunters.

She picked up the shotgun, untied the reins, and led the horse out of the trees.

Ike Hinds reined in halfway down the street. His partner slid down off the horse's back. Hinds climbed down, sliding his rifle out of the sheath.

'That bastard's here somewhere,' he said.

Benteen took out his handgun. 'All I need is one clear shot. You remember, Ike, he's mine!'

'We got to find him first.'

Benteen smiled his yellow-toothed smile. 'I got me a notion where he is!'

★　★　★

Seth and Alvin LeRoy had ridden hard for Bannock, both day and night, barely stopping, save for quick, cold meals. They were both tired and edgy by the time their horses took them down the trail that would bring them into town.

LeRoy, still weak from the bullet that had gone through his shoulder, had surprised Seth by his determination. He'd stayed in his saddle without once asking for help, though Seth had seen him sway limply a time or two. LeRoy was driven by a compunction that over-rode his physical condition.

It was LeRoy who spotted Hannah on the trail, leading a horse, a shotgun clasped in one hand.

They rode up to her and she turned suddenly, her eyes wide with alarm.

'I thought you were dead!' she said to LeRoy.

'Got to feeling that way myself a couple of times, ma'am,' LeRoy said. 'If it hadn't been for Marshal Tyler, here, I might just have been.'

'Tyler?' Hannah glanced up at Seth, seeing at once the likeness to Jacob. 'Are you Jacob's brother?'

'Seth.' He swung down out of the saddle. 'Where is he?'

'He went looking for Will Retford.'

'Will's here? In Bannock?'

Hannah nodded. 'Yes. He's the law here. Calls himself Will Ford!'

'Damnation!' Seth swung round on LeRoy. 'Facts, marshal! Cold, hard facts!'

LeRoy climbed down off his horse. 'Like I said, Tyler, if I'm proved wrong I'll be the first to apologise.' He glanced up the street. 'Is this Retford in town now?'

'I don't know,' Hannah said. 'Jacob went looking for him. That was an hour ago. Since then I haven't heard a thing.' Hannah suddenly reached out and clasped Seth's arm. 'My God! I almost forgot! The bounty-hunters — Benteen and Hinds. They rode in a few minutes ago. They're up in town now, and they'll be looking for Jacob!'

And following on her words there came a sudden crackle of gunfire from up at the far end of town.

★ ★ ★

Jacob had chosen to step out of the jail as Benteen and Hinds came up the street. He knew the moment he walked to the edge of the boardwalk that they had seen him, and he knew, too, that there would be no walking out of this without gunplay. The bounty-hunters were after him, for without his body — dead or alive — they couldn't claim their bounty. The pair had followed him a long way and they wouldn't be giving up now.

Benteen was in front, a gun in his hand; almost in that instant Jacob thought I wonder where he got the gun from, for he'd taken Benteen's weapon from him back in the gully; it was one of those fleeting thoughts that seemed to create themselves out of nowhere at a time when concentration needs to be held fully on some other matter.

Benteen's partner, Hinds, was some yards beyond. He had a rifle, which he was carrying as if it were a walking stick, but Jacob knew that rifle was as ready to use as any he'd seen.

The distance was rapidly closing as Benteen moved up the street. A few more yards and he would have his range, and once he did he would start shooting.

Jacob stepped down off the board-walk. The second his feet touched the street he reached for the gun at his side, drew, cocked and fired in one fluid motion. The big Colt crashed out its sound, smoke and flame blossoming from the muzzle.

Benteen stopped in his tracks. Blood showed on his shirt, high up on his chest. For a moment it seemed he was going to fall, but with surprising agility he ran forward, bringing up his own gun. His left hand dragged back the hammer and he fired off all the chambers with a swift fanning action.

Jacob had dropped into a crouch as Benteen ran forward. He ignored the spray of wild shots and set himself to return the fire. He steadied the Colt, aimed quickly and fired two close shots into Benteen's body; this time there was no mistake; the bullets caught Benteen in the centre of the chest, one of them driving through his body and severing his spine; Benteen collapsed like a limp rag, his body flopping helplessly in the bloody dust beneath him.

In the brief time it took for the first exchange of fire, Ike Hinds turned and stepped up on the far boardwalk, taking cover behind a stack of empty crates. He swung up his rifle, aiming fast, and as Benteen crashed down into the dust, Hinds loosed off a shot at Jacob's crouching figure. He knew he'd missed the second he fired. His bullet kicked up dirt to one side of Jacob's running figure.

He was about to fire again when he caught sight of three figures running up the street. Hinds saw the girl who'd been with Jacob Tyler, and there was the U.S. marshal he'd shot and left for dead. The third man was a stranger to Hinds, but he wore a lawman's badge, too.

Hinds felt trapped. His partner was dead and he was on his own, and he didn't expect any kind of mercy from those out there.

An anger, a red, blazing anger rose up in him. He felt only a wild desire to kill them all, and without realising it he stood up, bringing his rifle to his shoulder.

As his finger pulled back on the trigger he heard a distant yell. Then he fired. He didn't hear the bullet slam into the boardwalk on the other side of the street, for the sound was drowned out by a booming roar, a sound that Hinds knew well. He turned his head and saw with shocked surprise the girl, a flame-spitting shotgun in her hands. And it was aimed at him.

It was the last thing Hinds saw, for the full charge from both barrels hit him then. He felt sudden, intense pain as his upper body was torn open by the blast. The force of the charge drove him back across the boardwalk, into and through the plate-glass window of a store. In the split-second before pain and shock rendered him unconscious, Hinds registered a final thought, which to him seemed worse than actually dying: Christ, shot by a damn woman!

When they were inside the jail LeRoy removed the manacles from Jacob and Hannah.

'You sure you want to do that?' Jacob asked.

LeRoy massaged his aching shoulder. 'Mister, if I had any doubts you'd be in one of those cells back there.'

'I already have been,' Jacob said dryly.

Hannah glanced across at him, his words reminding her of all that had happened since that day. The best thing seemed to be the fact that they'd met, and she didn't regret one thing that had taken place since.

'Will's not likely to give himself up and confess,' Jacob told LeRoy.

'It's something I had thought of.' LeRoy sat down. 'Miss, I'd be grateful for some of that coffee you've got brewing.'

Hannah poured him a mugful.

LeRoy glanced up at the wall-clock.

It was almost a half-hour past noon.

'You figure they'll show?' Seth had asked the question that was on all their minds.

'Maybe! Maybe not!' LeRoy shrugged.

Jacob threw him a hard glance which LeRoy failed to see, but which Hannah caught. She moved to his side and put a hand on his arm.

'Take it easy,' she said softly. 'He's on your side now. Don't go and sour him!'

Jacob glanced at her, then smiled. She was right. There was no point in keeping on at LeRoy. What was important now was that the marshal almost fully believed Jacob's story. All they needed was Will's admittance of guilt. Which was going to be a hard thing to get.

'Riders coming!' Seth said from the door. He stepped out onto the street and after a minute he came back. 'It's them. Badges shining like they were at a lawman's convention.'

Jacob stepped forward, but LeRoy was suddenly blocking his way.

'I'll deal with it, Tyler.'

LeRoy walked outside and stood on the boardwalk as Will and his bunch rode up to the jail. He watched Will closely, and noticed the resemblance to the Retfords he'd seen that day back at Blanco Station; it was another fact to strengthen Jacob Tyler's claim; but LeRoy needed more — he needed the words from Will Retford himself.

The posse reined in noisily, yet despite the air of recklessness, LeRoy was quick to notice the unease that clouded Will Retford's face; it showed in his eyes, too.

'You find him?' LeRoy asked.

Will leaned forward slighhtly. 'Who?'

'Tyler. Jacob Tyler. He's the one you've been looking for isn't it?'

'Who are you, mister?'

LeRoy eased his coat aside, exposing his badge. 'LeRoy's the name. U.S. Marshal Alvin LeRoy. Been after Tyler myself for some time now. Ever since that killing down at Blanco Station.'

'You turned up anything new on that?' Will asked.

LeRoy shook his head. 'Tyler's still claiming there was another man there that day. Says he did the shooting. Calls him Retford! Will Retford!'

Will's face paled visibly. In his eyes was mounting fear; he was beginning to panic; LeRoy realised he was on the right track.

'He'll be claiming he didn't do the holdups and killings up here,' Will said, trying to push the conversation on; yet while he spoke his mind was whirling as he tried to visualise his next step. 'Even though he's killed the one witness we had, and two of my deputies.'

LeRoy didn't answer and silence dragged on for a moment. He could almost see Will sweating; the man was undecided what to do; he was tense and getting close to the edge.

Over his shoulder LeRoy called: 'In the jail! Step out here.'

Will shot a startled glance towards the jail door, and saw three figures step out into the sunlight.

'That's him, Marshal. Will Retford,'

Jacob said. 'He's the one who shot Nancy Boland! And he can tell you how Virgil Boone died!'

At Jacob's side stood Seth. 'Jacob's right, LeRoy. This is Retford!'

And then there was Hannah, moving forward to stand beside Jacob. 'You look into it, Marshal, I think you'll find he knows more about these holdups than he and his men would admit to!'

Hannah's words seemed to be the final accusation, and Will knew there would be no talking his way out of this. This time there was no running away from it. Will knew that if he wanted to come out of this a free man he was going to have to fight for his freedom.

'Gun 'em!' he yelled. 'It's us or them, and I don't figure to end up in a cell.'

Will's voice rose to a scream of rage as he made a grab for his gun. Around him his deputies, realising their days were numbered if they didn't move fast, followed suit.

Bannock's main street was suddenly alive with the sound of gunfire. Horses screamed in fright, rearing and stamping in panic. The smell of burnt powder was heavy. From beneath trampling hooves dust rose in stinging clouds.

It was a fight in which the steady eye and hand scored over the quick, thoughtless shot. Within seconds there were a number of empty saddles as Jacob, Seth and Alvin LeRoy returned the deputies' fire.

Of them all only Jacob sought a particular target. And to his frustration was the fact that Will Retford seemed to have vanished. Jacob swore angrily. So close, and now Will had vanished again!

As the rattle of gunfire died down, Jacob heard a drum of hooves on the street. He ran along the boardwalk until he was clear of the milling horses and swirling dust. And across the other side of the street he saw Will, aiming his trotting horse towards the other end of town and the open road.

Jacob ran across the street. He ran faster than he'd ever done before, or ever wanted to again. All he could see was Will, and Will was running. Jacob had no intention of letting that happen. Not this time. He'd gone through too much to have it come to nothing.

He was only yards away from Will's horse when Will turned his head. And the first thing Will saw was Jacob. A scream of rage rose up in Will's throat as he laid his eyes on Jacob. He swung his gun round, tipping the muzzle down at Jacob's weaving figure. Will fired, two quick shots that missed Jacob by inches, plowing into the ground.

Before Will could fire again Jacob was onto him. He reached up and grabbed Will's gunhand, dragging Will bodily out of the saddle. Will hit the ground hard, his gun spilling from his fingers. He kicked out wildly. Jacob was thrust aside by a blow that slammed his left side. As he regained his balance Will came to his feet and threw himself at Jacob. They came together hard, trading powerful, crippling blows to face and body. They ignored the pain, the blood that poured from them; they were men fighting on emotions;- for Jacob it was a cleansing of all the hardship and misery he'd gone through because of this man, and the hurt he'd suffered through Nancy's death; Will had taken her life and Jacob wanted him to suffer for that; it was plain and simple vengeance. For Will it was simply a fight for life, his life; if he lost here today he was going to pay with his life; he knew now that given time it would all come out; the planned holdups he and his bunch had pulled; the killings; the corruption of the office of marshal; Will didn't fool himself; if they got him to court he'd end up with a noose around his neck.

They fought without feeling or mercy. They moved off the boardwalk where they'd knocked themselves, back on to the street, slipping and stumbling with exhaustion, but neither of them giving an inch. Pounding, gouging, punching, each tried to destroy the other.

And then Will found himself on his back. High above him he could see the blue sky. It appeared to be spinning and the brightness hurt his eyes. His body seemed to be one mass of pain. He could taste blood in his mouth. There was a dull pain in his chest that hurt each time he took a breath.

Tyler had beaten him! The fact hammered in his mind. They would take him and put him in a cell now. And when all the talking was over they would take him out one morning and they would hang him. A cold knot formed in his stomach. The Hell they would! He wasn't finished completely yet.

The marshal, LeRoy, pulled him to his feet. Will stood for a moment, trying to clear his fogged senses.

'Let's go, mister,' LeRoy said.

They started across the street. Jacob Tyler was a few yards ahead, the girl by his side.

As they reached the far side of the street they had to pass a parked wagon. The wagon belonged to a local rancher. The tailgate was down and Will's eyes caught sight of a double-edged axe lying in the wagon. As he stepped by the wagon he reached out and grabbed the axe. Summoning his strength Will swung the axe up and brought it round at LeRoy's head.

It never landed.

Close by a gun fired. Two quick, close shots, the hard sound slamming out loudly. Will was driven back by the impact of two heavy bullets ripping into his chest, tearing through flesh and bone. They left large, jagged wounds where they emerged between his shoulder-blades. Blood fountained in a bright spray as Will struck the side of the wagon and pitched face down on the ground.

By the time Jacob reached him Will was barely breathing. Jacob turned him over. Will was losing a lot of blood. He glanced at Jacob's bruised and bloody face.

'You put those bullets in me?' Will asked.

'No. I did!' Will glanced at the speaker

and saw Seth Tyler looking down at him.

'Damn you to Hell!' Will shouted, then felt his body shudder as it was racked with pain; he began to cough, blood spilling from his lips. The wounds in his chest were bleeding badly too, and Will could feel his grip on life slipping away fast; he'd made one mistake too many this time; despite everything Will Retford was no fool; he was dying and he knew it.

'You put yourself on the line,' Jacob said.

Will glanced at him. 'Yeah. Well I ain't exactly laughin' about it myself.'

'It might have ended differently,' Jacob said, 'if you hadn't run. It just made trouble all the way round.'

'Ain't no good thinkin' on that now. Man does what he thinks is the best way out. I figured it was all up when that girl caught my bullet. What with the Law around and all, I decided the best thing was to get the Hell out.'

LeRoy leaned closer to ask: 'Who

killed the deputy marshal?'

Will's bloody lips peeled back in a thin smile. 'That's the best part about it, Marshal. It was an accident. Your deputy was shot with his own gun while he was trying to keep the girl off him. She wouldn't let go and the gun went off!' Will began to laugh, the sound deep and ragged. 'All this time, LeRoy, you've been chasin' an innocent man. There never was any murder! Man, that makes it almost worthwhile dyin' for. Just to see your face!'

His laughter rose until it was almost too loud. Then just as abruptly it was cut off. Will began to gasp for breath, his face darkening as he began to choke. He started coughing up dark blood and his body stiffened, arching violently. And in moments it was over.

Jacob stood up. He sensed someone watching him and when he turned he saw it was LeRoy.

'I was wrong, Tyler,' he said. 'More wrong than a man has a right to be in my job. I can only say you'll have no more trouble from me.'

LeRoy held out his hand and Jacob, after only the slightest hesitation, took it in his own.

'LeRoy, you just keep wearing that badge. This country needs good lawmen, and I figure any man is entitled to one mistake. Hell, I've made my share, and I don't reckon I've done yet!'

'What will you do now?'

Jacob drew Hannah close. He indicated the ragged remainders of Will's gang. 'We'll give you a hand to tidy this mess up,' he said. 'Then Seth and me and Hannah — why I reckon we're going home!'

THE END

We do hope that you have enjoyed reading this large print book.

Did you know that all of our titles are available for purchase?

We publish a wide range of high quality large print books including:
Romances, Mysteries, Classics General Fiction Non Fiction and Westerns

Special interest titles available in large print are:
The Little Oxford Dictionary Music Book, Song Book Hymn Book, Service Book

Also available from us courtesy of Oxford University Press:
Young Readers' Dictionary (large print edition) Young Readers' Thesaurus (large print edition)

For further information or a free brochure, please contact us at:
Ulverscroft Large Print Books Ltd., The Green, Bradgate Road, Anstey, Leicester, LE7 7FU, England. Tel: (00 44) **0116 236 4325 Fax:** (00 44) **0116 234 0205**